Praise for *The Adventures of Miles and Isabel:*

"*The Adventures of Miles and Isabel* is a novel of dreams and fantasy and not a little theatricality, all solidly rooted in honest scientific inquiry and experimentation. . . . [Gilling] has an appealing comic flair. . . . [He] makes readers want to believe in dreams and love—and gives us every reason to do so."
—David Willis McCullough, *The New York Times Book Review*

"A pretty tale of a young man filled with dreams and daring, and a young woman of strong will and unconventional behavior."
—Barbara Fisher, *The Boston Globe*

"Fantastical and magical, this novel is peppered with humor and the excitement of a time period laden with anticipation and opportunities for the creative, restless minds of innovation."   —*Booklist*

"A delightful second novel . . . Rich and amiable, with a fresh wit and a good eye for history."   —*Kirkus Reviews*

"Wonderful and magical . . . A great book for all collections."
—*Library Journal*

"Delightful."   —*Bookseller* (UK)

"This is not romance but Romance, the medieval genre that's not concerned, like the conventional novel, with minute fidelity to the real world, but with life transfigured with enchantment, the mundane and the mysterious alchemically mixed. . . . Gilling's interleaved tales are told with such ease and lightness of touch it's as if he's narrating an existing legend that's been retold over and over, with every excess word worn away. . . . The characters live and kick, and the detail is unfailingly deft."
—Barry Oakley, *The Bulletin* (Australia)

"Hugely enjoyable and memorable."
—Diana Simmonds, *Good Reading Magazine* (Australia)

"[*The Adventures of Miles and Isabel*] works as a novel not just because of the strength and unpredictability of its two central characters; . . . as it plays with history and technology, it finds copious other material with which to engage." —Michael McGirr, *Sydney Morning Herald* (Australia)

"Gilling weaves [*The Adventures of Miles and Isabel*] together with seamless ease. The prose is such a delight to read, I was tempted to backtrack, trying to work out how so much could be achieved with so little apparent effort. . . . Tom Gilling is a naturally gifted writer. He celebrates imagination. Highly recommended."
—Ian McFarlane, *Canberra Times* (Australia)

"There are echoes here of Angela Carter's classic *Nights at the Circus* and Paul Auster's *Mr. Vertigo*. Hot on the heels of his well-loved first novel, *The Sooterkin*, Gilling again produces the goods—a compelling mix of quirky characters, whimsy and a soupcon of magic." —*Qantas* (Australia)

"Gilling shares with his central characters a longing to soar, if only off the page, and he rides his galloping prose with an unmitigated sense of confidence and freedom." —Jen Vuk, *The Big Issue* (UK)

"[*The Adventures of Miles and Isabel*] would be a pretty ordinary, predictable little love story if it weren't so adroitly told. But somehow Gilling manages to lift it into the air, creating a narrative that is as seamless and full of puff as a well-made sail in high wind. . . . Tom Gilling has now proved himself an exceptionally talented novelist twice over." —Cameron Woodhead, *The Age* (Australia)

"[*The Adventures of Miles and Isabel*] is a rarity: a novel that combines history and fantasy in a fluent, witty manner that never seems to strain for effect but constantly surprises with its twists of plot and subplot. . . . It is one of the most memorably entertaining Australian novels . . . and the book is laden with sheer delight."—Michael Sharkey, *Weekend Australian*

The Adventures
of
Miles and Isabel

The Adventures
of
Miles and Isabel

TOM GILLING

Grove Press
New York

First published in 2001 in Australia by The Text Publishing Company, Melbourne, Australia

Published simultaneously in Canada

Printed in the United States of America

FIRST GROVE PRESS EDITION

Library of Congress Cataloging-in-Publication Data

Gilling, Tom.

    [Miles McGinty]

    The adventures of Miles and Isabel / Tom Gilling.

    p. cm.

    Originally published under title: Miles McGinty. Melbourne, Vic. : Text Pub., c2001.

    ISBN 0-8021-4019-X (pbk.)

    1. Australia—Fiction. 2. Air pilots—Fiction. 3. Levitation—Fiction. 4. Inventors—Fiction. I. Title.

    PR9619.3.G538 M35 2002

    823'.914—dc21   2002016414

The author gratefully acknowledges the assistance of the Commonwealth Government through the Australia Council, its arts funding and advisory body.

Grove Press

841 Broadway

New York, NY 10003

03 04 05 06 07 10 9 8 7 6 5 4 3 2 1

for
Rosemary

Harry Brutus Fitzpatrick lay sprawled on the stage of the Prince of Wales theatre, his tiny slippered feet protruding like asparagus tips from the hem of a black fur coat. A purple scar embossed his right cheek: an arc that stretched from his eyebrow to his chin and parodied the scowl that was a fixture on his lips. Fitzpatrick was a better actor than a swordsman, though these days that wasn't saying much. Beside him stood an empty bottle of whisky, one of a pair he had smuggled into his dressing room the previous night.

'Who spoke to him last?' asked Hope Wentworth, the impresario whose wallet had brought Fitzpatrick out of a baleful retirement. He believed that a great actor was never finished until he was dead, and truly great actors survived even that.

'He collared me as I was locking up,' said the caretaker, hovering over the fallen tragedian with his mop.

'Did he seem anxious?'

'Drunk is what I'd call it.'

Now and again Fitzpatrick would lock himself in a hotel room, refusing to emerge until he'd emptied a couple of bottles of cheap whisky. He would come out trembling and confused, red-eyed, unshaven but as arrogant as ever, hunting for some hapless passer-by to vent his anger on. Gradually the confinements had become longer, the tantrums more pathetic, until there wasn't a manager in New South Wales who would hire him. Then, in early 1856, Wentworth had taken it upon himself to revive the actor's career during the coming winter in Sydney. Wentworth's plan was to ease Fitzpatrick back in some telling but not-too-onerous Shakespearian role: Malvolio, perhaps, or Enobarbus. Fitzpatrick had rejected both. It would be Hamlet or nothing.

'Should be bloody ashamed of hisself,' growled the caretaker. 'Who is he anyway?'

Wentworth sat down on a fallen battlement. His eyes grew moist at the thought of the two hundred guineas it would cost him to cancel. The cast had already been decimated by a bout of flu. Several names had been scratched from the poster. The survivors stood on stage gazing at the supine figure whose coat, they noticed, was flecked with vomit. It was ten minutes past four; the doors opened at seven.

Wentworth liked actors but had learned not to trust them. Now he was throwing himself on their mercy. He turned to the American, Mr Schwartz, who had helped him out of many a scrape but was no more capable of acting the part of Hamlet than the caretaker. Before Schwartz could offer his advice a woman's voice said, 'Let me do it.'

The speaker was Eliza McGinty.

'You?'

'I haven't seen anyone else volunteering.'

Mr Delillo, whose meagre talents were strained in the role of the second gravedigger, began to raise his hand but changed his mind.

'She knows it backwards, dear,' said Mrs Gwilym, the oldest member of the company. She glanced at Fitzpatrick, who hadn't moved. 'I'll bet she knows it better than himself.'

Wentworth looked around, convinced he was having his leg pulled.

Eliza was gloriously pregnant, as pregnant as any woman could be while still standing on her feet. In the last month she had swelled up like a balloon. Her graceful walk had become a waddle.

'There won't be an empty seat,' said Eliza.

'It'll be a scandal,' said Mrs Gwilym. 'The papers will love it.'

'Of course I appreciate…' Wentworth began.

'Oh bollocks, dear,' said Mrs Gwilym. 'It's that or give them their money back.'

It was a big enough risk, Wentworth thought, to allow a woman in Eliza's state to play Ophelia. He felt an awful foreboding but could think of no alternative. 'Who will do Ophelia?' he asked.

Mrs Gwilym had done her first Ophelia at seventeen and saw no reason to stop now she was sixty.

Wentworth stared at Eliza and shook his shaggy head. 'You can wear a cloak,' he said. 'There's no need to flaunt it.'

Fitzpatrick gurgled and rolled over.

⌒

Eliza McGinty's beauty was compelling from the stalls, indisputable from the upper circle, but sometimes open to unkind scrutiny from the mob in the pit. She was a big-hearted woman with big bones to match. Audiences admired her not for the deftness of her talent, but for the size of it. Eliza did not disappoint them. She gave them grand gestures and volcanic passions; her sobs shook the boxes; her dying breath startled horses in the street.

At the age of thirty-three, she had found herself pregnant. The child's father, a whippet-waisted scene-shifter, had guessed the story and shot through, leaving a pound note, a winter coat and two pairs of coloured silk stockings.

'Pretty stockings,' remarked Mrs Gwilym. 'Must have cost a few shillings.' She had borne several children to several men and hadn't felt it worth her while to stay in touch with any of them.

'Take them,' said Eliza. 'I won't have 'em.'

She had expected her lover back and was miserable when he failed to appear. 'I know a lady, dear,' said Mrs Gwilym, seeing her puke one morning into a bucket. 'She is not expensive.' She added casually, 'I once had to use her myself.'

Eliza had not chosen to conceive. More than once she considered getting rid of the baby, but she couldn't bring herself to do it. As the months passed, and it made its presence felt, her attachment grew until she found herself stroking her belly in bed, cooing, even reading the newspaper aloud. As she swelled, her voice grew, her presence expanded. Harry Brutus Fitzpatrick, who once bestrode the stage from Muswellbrook to Mildura, hesitated to appear with her at less than twice his usual fee.

Watching the sentinels stumble through their opening routine ('Get thee to bed, Francisco…For this relief much thanks. 'Tis bitter cold'), Eliza felt something she hadn't felt in years: palpitations, cramps clawing at her, a spasm that reminded her of the days when the sight of an audience made her heart race. She perched on the edge of a piano stool, her huge stomach and breasts enveloped in a velvet cape, and hugged the fidgeting child inside her.

~

Eliza had often seen a tremor pass through an audience at the start of Hamlet's famous soliloquy. It was most conspicuous in the expensive seats and signalled a brief period of alertness before torpor resumed. But tonight there wasn't an ear at any price that didn't hang on her every word. 'To be, or not to be,' she whispered, 'that is the question.'

The play was into its second week and there was hardly an empty seat in the house —apart from the one in Box A reserved for Harry Brutus Fitzpatrick, who had not been seen by any member of the company since his meeting with Wentworth the morning after Eliza's debut. The *Sydney Morning Herald*, the *Illustrated Sydney News* and the *Australian* had all denounced Mrs McGinty's 'scandalous Hamlet' while bemoaning the loss of 'the gifted but temperamental Mr Fitzpatrick'. But none denied the steely conviction of her performance or the elfin curiosity of Mrs Gwilym's Ophelia.

In the better suburbs of Sydney strings were being pulled and debts called in for the sake of a ticket. In Stanmore, in a red-brick mansion overlooking the railway line, Ernest Dowling bowed reluctantly to the demands of his wife, Louisa, for a seat as close to the front of the dress circle as a merchant banker's money could buy.

'Is it entirely sensible, my love,' muttered Dowling, 'in your condition?'

Dowling was a faithful husband but not an enthusiastic one. He had experienced no sexual urges at all until the age of twenty-eight. Even then they were so vague as to be indistinguishable from the feelings aroused by a bottle of hock. His virility was a source of quiet mortification to him. He had never found his wife particularly attractive, though he was aware that other men did, and he didn't object. She was small and birdlike and an excellent cards player.

Louisa Dowling was an aficionado of the stage, a fervent admirer of Mrs McGinty. She'd supposed that Harry Brutus Fitzpatrick was dead and was glad for his sake that he wasn't. But it was Eliza she wanted to see.

'We've been through this already, Ernest,' she said, meaning that she had declared her intention to go and Dowling had understood the impossibility of talking her out of it.

'Of course,' he admitted. 'Only…'

'Only nothing, dear. Society has not banned the bearing of children and if it's uncomfortable with the consequences then it has only to avert its eyes. If Mrs McGinty can play Hamlet in her condition, I'm sure she won't be offended if I watch her in mine.'

Dowling conceded defeat with a roll of his eyes, piercingly blue in his youth, now a rather turbid grey. It was not Mrs McGinty's taking offence that bothered him. Nor, despite his conservative instincts, was he greatly concerned by what society might think. But he felt that once a woman reached a certain point in her pregnancy she should withdraw to the comfort of her own home, lie on a sofa and wait for the inevitable to happen. And Mrs Dowling, he felt, was at or very near that point.

Eliza could guess at such conversations from the snatches she caught from crowds in the street. A mob had gathered each day outside the stage door, one half chiding and the other begging for her autograph.

'Ay,' she continued, looking up at the boxes, 'there's the rub.' A sudden contraction made her wince. She had to steady herself against a wall.

The bulldog-faced critic from the *Illustrated Sydney News*, who had been pointed out to her on the first night, was crouching again at the front of the stalls. A short bald man was sitting beside him, sketching in a pad. His head nestled like an alabaster egg in the upturned collar of his woollen overcoat. Eliza had amused herself by refusing to stand still, turning her head whenever she spotted him hunched over his pad. Now she stared at him, her face contorted in pain.

'Soft you now,' she whispered, catching sight of Mrs Gwilym, her face so thickly caked in powder that her cheeks had begun to fissure, 'the fair Ophelia!'

The line was met, as always, by hoots of laughter from the pit. But Mrs Gwilym, professional to the soles of her dancing pumps, was unperturbed. She gazed down on her mockers as if to remind them that anything cheaper than the one and six-pennies was beneath her notice and her contempt. 'Good my lord,' she croaked, 'How does your honour for this many a day?'

Eliza caught the little wink that signified the older woman's indifference to the catcalls flying around her ears. Her contractions, however, were becoming worse. Anxious faces were watching her from the wings.

'O woe is me,' Mrs Gwilym wailed as Eliza sank to her knees, 'T'have seen what I have seen, see what I see.'

In the second row of the dress circle Mrs Ernest Dowling was feeling queasy. Not enough to regret coming, but more than enough to wish she had insisted on a private box. Dowling sat beside her, aware that his wife was in some discomfort and dimly apprehensive of the consequences.

An empty seat to Mrs Dowling's left saved her from having to keep her bearskin coat on her lap. It was cold outside but the gaslights and tobacco smoke made the theatre stuffy. She flapped herself with the program.

'Are you quite certain...' ventured Dowling, who would rather not have come but could never think of an excuse when one was needed.

'Hush, Ernest,' she whispered.

Her concern for Mrs McGinty, who was being helped to her feet, distracted her from the dull ache in her lower back, a pain identical to those that had preceded the births of all her five daughters. Each had been born exactly eighteen months after her predecessor, giving Louisa a year or so to enjoy the slender figure that still made her look ten years younger than she was. Rosalind, Olivia, Jane, Emily and Helena had all ripened and dropped as predictably as the cumquats in the greenhouse—and always on a Wednesday. Mrs Dowling never felt the first pains until every household chore had been done, every tradesman paid off and everyone visited who needed visiting. She did not expect to give birth for another fortnight and dismissed the pain as a phantom that would go away if she ignored it.

Several more scenes passed. Louisa felt her attention come and go, more or less in time with the ache in her back. As the gravediggers jested over their shovels Louisa was conscious of a soft moaning in the wings. The obvious suspect, a bald ghost in a rusty breastplate, had retreated several scenes before to his dressing room. This, in any case, was a woman's voice.

At first the gravediggers pretended nothing was happening. But the moan grew louder, causing several gentlemen in the front row of the circle to stand up. Others jumped up behind them. A program-seller who had been annoying patrons in the aisle seats called for a doctor.

'Eliza, dear,' hissed the first gravedigger, 'is that you?'

Eliza, with Mr Delillo under one arm and Mrs Gwilym under the other, looked down to see a puddle spreading between her feet.

In the second row of the dress circle Mr Dowling alone stayed glued to his seat. He didn't pretend to understand the theatre; he went merely to accompany his wife, who (he now noticed) was neither sitting nor standing but squatting and uttering noises that seemed to echo those coming from the stage, though so softly that they could scarcely be heard above the din.

Louisa Dowling's feelings were no less strong for being suggestible. She suffered the torments of every Hamlet who had ever walked on stage. On moonlit nights she could see the ghost of her own father clanking in his armour before her eyes. In her fragile state the sound of another woman entering labour was all she needed to set her off.

Dowling leaned over. He allowed himself the rare familiarity of putting a hand on her wrist. He said, 'Are you quite certain…'

'Take me home,' whispered Louisa. 'Hurry!'

Ernest Dowling sat at the foot of the stairs and listened with equanimity to the fearful sounds that his wife, in the course of five deliveries, had raised to a pitch of dramatic perfection. He wore his slippers and a three-quarter-length velvet smoking jacket, though out of sympathy for her ordeal he didn't smoke. Now and then he stood up, startled out of his newspaper by a few seconds' unexpected silence, refusing to resume his seat until someone had been sent in to find out what progress (if any) had been made.

Just before dawn on Sunday morning a baby girl flopped onto the crumpled sheets of a fat four-poster in the red-brick mansion overlooking the railway line. She was pug-faced with green eyes and a frown that seemed to dart about the room, demanding answers. Her mother named her Isabel.

At that moment, in an upstairs room at the front of the Orient Hotel, Eliza McGinty clutched to her breast the long-limbed boy she'd been pushing out since the curtains dropped prematurely in the Prince of Wales theatre.

The landlord, John Fogerty, was an old friend of Eliza's who had once been much more. He thought no less of her for there being no Mr McGinty and wrote in the register, since she was in no state to write it herself, the words 'Eliza McGinty, widow'.

The full moon hung as fat as a pudding over Sydney Harbour. Its reflection, a buttery slick stirred here and there by lighters and lobstermen's boats, lapped at the wharves. A yellowish fog sweated over the roof of the Orient Hotel.

'What are you calling him?' asked Mrs Gwilym, whose coolness towards her own offspring didn't preclude an interest in other people's. She was still in costume, her white sleeves now stained with blood.

'I haven't chosen a name,' said Eliza.

Mrs Gwilym nodded. 'One'll come to you,' she said. 'They always do.' She seemed about to launch into the story of how her own children were named, but wandered instead to the open window and stood gazing into the dawn.

Eliza's baby was strong and dark, with a head of hair that already needed cutting. Thinking of how far she had carried him, she called him Miles.

In his first year he travelled to Yass and Gulgong and Tamworth and Bathurst, stopping at smaller towns along the way, once venturing as far as Albury on the New South Wales side of the Murray River. His view of the world was a dusty square of blue sky framed by the window of a leather-sprung Cobb & Co. coach. He was two and a half before he was tall enough to see the country outside.

Miles's career began at the age of three, trotting on stage whenever the play called for a child to be sung to or cooed over, and hugging his mother's calves as coins and bouquets showered from the boxes during curtain calls.

With Wentworth's company they toured the Victorian goldfields, where drunken miners pelted the stage with paper pouches of gold dust and nuggets wrapped in handkerchiefs. They did a shipwreck in Wagga Wagga and mounted the fall of Sebastopol in Shepparton.

Miles was not big-boned and plump, like his mother. His legs were long and thin, his hips sharp, his shoulders narrow. With his olive skin, he was like the negative of the sallow father he had never seen, and who had never seen him. He had dark deep-set eyes, and black hair that resisted all his mother's efforts to brush it.

He scrambled up high ladders without a trace of fear. Mr Delillo, reduced by now to the role of costume manager, taught him the name of every cloud in the sky. A month short of his fourth birthday, Eliza caught him swinging from the roof of the Royal Victoria Theatre in Sydney. A stagehand named Govett had put him there, strapping him into the same leather harness in which Mrs Gwilym, now retired, had performed her famous Puck a quarter of a century earlier.

Eliza's heart froze at the sight of him dangling above the stage. 'Miles, come down,' she shouted.

'Never mind him,' said Govett. 'The young feller ain't even nervous.' He was pulling muscatels from a paper bag, biting them whole and scratching the seeds out of his teeth with his thumbnail.

'Maybe not, Mr Govett, but his mother is,' said Eliza, who couldn't help admiring Miles's grace and lack of fear.

'I've seen paid-up flymen without his pluck,' said Govett. He was an old Irishman who'd learnt his trade in the Dublin theatres and had seen many a man break an arm or leg falling out of the flies. 'Fancy a muscat, love?'

'Fetch him down at once, and don't put him up there again.'

'He don't need the likes of me to get him up,' said Govett, reaching carelessly into his bag. 'Climbs like a spider, that one.'

Miles swung back and forth in his harness while the stagehand hauled him in with a block and tackle.

Eliza slapped him hard behind the knees; for disobedience, she said, and so he'd know what to expect next time. Miles refused to cry. When he lay in bed that night she pulled the blankets right up to his chin, tugging the corners tight as if she feared he'd float away without them. He wasn't theatrical like she was; he'd fly just as happily in an empty room. But there was some of her daring in him, a courage that both excited and alarmed her.

Isabel did not like dolls. She didn't like them because she had so many, and because none of them were hers. They reached her, along with her pram and her pinafores and her miniature leather boots, from one or more of her older sisters; sometimes from all five. Most of them were presents from their grandmother, a stout silver-haired old lady who spoke to her cats as though they were bridge partners.

Nobody expected Isabel to love her pinafores but they did expect her to love her dolls, even if they weren't really hers. When she was old enough to resent the chips and scratches, and to recognise the wistful looks they still got from her sisters, she turned their heads to the wall and stopped talking to them. Her mother would dutifully rearrange them, huddling them together in intimate groups, knitting them scarves, giving them new names. Then they began to disappear, one by one, in such a way that their individual absences took some time to become obvious. On the eve of her sixth birthday, the gardener dug one up among the parsnips. Isabel's pretended delight was so convincing, even to her mother, that no-one hesitated to blame the dog—a clever English terrier—or asked how the doll came to be wrapped in a shroud. But none was ever found again, and Isabel quickly turned her interest to books.

Mr Dowling, realising with relief that this child was to be his last, took her shopping one Saturday afternoon in Castlereagh Street. She was seven, a pretty green-eyed girl whose long hair refused to sit under the wide-brimmed hat that her mother had pinned to it.

Dowling loved all his daughters when they were small. He enjoyed their attempts to speak, their exuberant mimicry, their comical mistakes. As each one grew older he found her chatter less rewarding and transferred his affections discreetly to her successor. Their swelling bodies, on the rare occasions he saw them, made him blush.

Isabel had no successor. It didn't take her long to grasp the nature of her advantage. 'This one,' she cried, pointing to a dubious shop crushed between a haberdashery store on one side and a hotel on the other.

'I don't think so, Isabel,' said Dowling. 'It's…' He wasn't certain what it was. There were a few books in the window in scruffy leather bindings, some scrimshaw teeth, a tray of gold rings. Deeper inside the shop, bits and pieces of shoddy furniture, more books spilling out of a camphorwood chest, some old etchings and faded watercolours on the walls. There was nothing new and unowned, the qualities Dowling looked for in a purchase. It would no more have entered his head to go inside than it would have to drink at the bar next door. But before he could draw her away, the little brass bell above the door tinkled and Isabel was grinning back at him through the window.

Dowling had intended to buy her a pair of gloves: expensive English pigskin. There was, he thought, something fetching about a little girl in gloves. He was prepared to spend five guineas, twice what he'd spend on himself. He felt uncomfortable, not to say itchy, surrounded by other people's possessions.

'That's what I want,' said Isabel. Her father had taken her hand and she had taken it back.

'I don't think so, dear.' He didn't bother to look at her find, or at the shopkeeper who had been dozing on his counter and was now awake and rubbing his nose with the back of his hand. Isabel could have walked around the shop pointing to any object at random and heard from her father the same five words. He was a man of unerring consistency. Isabel turned away, as if to look at something else, then immediately came back to her original choice, a florid statuette of a man and his dog entitled '*Le balloniste et son chien*'. It was about nine inches tall, and was poorly cast out of inferior brass full of pock holes. Dowling's French was adequate to translate the accompanying label which identified the subject as Francois Pilatre de Rozier, who in October 1783 made the first manned flight in a hot-air balloon, reaching a height of eighty-two feet in a Montgolfiere secured by cables. The sculptor was anonymous.

'But...' he began to protest.

'The doggy,' said Isabel, 'he looks just like Bethsheba.' The dog did, in fact, resemble the red setter that Dowling bought for his wife soon after the birth of their first daughter. Bethsheba had been killed two years earlier after running onto the railway line. She'd been replaced by the black and brindle terrier that now spent its life burying beef bones in the vegetable garden and exhuming them, black and crawling with maggots, for presentation to guests after Sunday lunch.

'That hardly seems a good reason,' continued her father.

'You said you'd buy me a present.'

'And I will, dear. Only—'

'I want it, Papa.'

'Please don't stamp your foot.'

'It's only four guineas.'

'The price, Isabel, is not the issue.'

'Will you buy it or won't you?'

The shopkeeper, watching from behind the counter, understood that it was not in his interests to intervene.

'My dear Isabel, I really think your mother—'

'It's not for her. Please, Papa.'

Dowling feared his daughters' tantrums more, even, than he feared their bodies. Isabel's were particularly terrible as they happened so suddenly and were so shameless. It would have been quite within her powers to collapse on the shopkeeper's floor and refuse to get up. Worse things had been reported by her mother. Dowling would then have to surrender to his daughter as well as offer a humiliating excuse to a stranger. He insisted on having the statue wrapped and tied with string and put in a bag that would betray no hint of its contents. The shopkeeper stood at the window and watched them go, sniffing and rubbing his nose with the hand that wasn't fingering his four guineas.

As Isabel and her father emerged from the shop, a swollen-bellied mule tore herself at last from the water trough outside the Victoria Barracks and set off down the hill towards Hyde Park. Her owner was nowhere in sight. The animal did not take the most direct route, which would have led her down Oxford Street, over Liverpool Street and anticlockwise around the perimeter of the park. Instead she turned left, down one of the lanes that tumbled into Elizabeth Street, stopping at intervals to relieve the pressure on her bladder, until she found herself part of a big crowd converging on the place where Tobias Smith, a haberdasher's assistant, was standing in a baker's basket festooned with ribbons. Isabel and Mr Dowling heard the hubbub as they walked up Liverpool Street.

Smith was an employee in the firm of Swedenborg & Co. of Castlereagh Street. He was twenty-two and good-looking in a pale, undernourished sort of way that suggested far too much of his income had gone into his patent leather shoes. He had been standing still for several minutes, inclining his head now and then in the direction of an unaccompanied lady, of whom there were many.

'You see, Papa,' said Isabel, 'I told you it hasn't a driver.'

They had been walking around the shops for an hour. Isabel had relinquished the bag hiding her brass sculpture, which Mr Dowling was now carrying, his arm thrust out as if the bag contained a poisoned rat.

Dowling had seen the crowds and done his best to entice Isabel into a cab that would take them home. He remembered (too late) reading an article in the *Sydney Morning Herald* announcing the attempt on Saturday afternoon by a man called Smith to become Australia's first balloonist. By and large he had no interest in men called Smith. He had no interest in balloons. It would have been enough for him to read about them over breakfast in the *Sydney Morning Herald*.

Isabel was too young to read the newspaper. But she loved a spectacle as much as her father hated it. And it was, after all, Isabel's day out. She had anticipated his resistance and found endless ways of frustrating it. The latest was the swollen-bellied mule ambling up the middle of Elizabeth Street minus its owner. Her father had pointed out, in his managerial way, several possible reasons for this. Isabel listened to each one before listing her objections. These were numerous enough to deliver them to the gates of Hyde Park.

'We are here now, Papa,' she said, gripping the iron railings with both hands. 'Please can't we go in?'

'What about the mule?' Dowling asked.

'What mule?' said Isabel.

Gustav Swedenborg was a big man with boar bristles on his cheeks. He kept a stock of hatbands to rival anything in London or Paris and spent the greater part of his day with his hands behind his back, pacing up and down before a cabinet of coloured threads said to be the largest in the southern hemisphere. Customers came from as far away as Newcastle and Katoomba to draw on his expertise in ribbons and fastenings. Some of them were among the hordes streaming into Hyde Park on this balmy April afternoon to see Tobias Smith hoisted a thousand feet over Sydney in a hot-air balloon.

Swedenborg stood beside the basket with his hands clasped behind his back, nodding smugly from time to time and doing his best to convince the crowd that he was as much a part of the great adventure as his employee—more, in fact, since he had subscribed two hundred and fifty guineas towards the cost of the balloon.

Other members of the syndicate stood nearby, radiant with their contribution to the enterprise of dragging New South Wales into the age of flight. A praetorian guard of short fat top-hatted industrialists ringed the basket so tightly that it seemed they would have to be jettisoned one by one along with the sandbags if the balloon was ever to get off the ground.

There was one gap, left by a trader in chicken feed who had fallen unexpectedly ill with diphtheria. His place was taken by a placard that said:

Children of New South Wales
Step Inside the Basket if you Dare
TWO SHILLINGS will Buy your Place in History

The majority understood the invitation for what it was: a shabby attempt by the syndicate to recoup some of its investment from a public that had already been fleeced of a shilling to enter the park. There were few takers. The odd small boy had succeeded in extorting two shillings from his father for the honour of being lowered into the basket and having his head patted by Tobias Smith. Most were content to gaze up at the straining balloon and rattle the ropes if they got the chance.

Ernest Dowling found himself and Isabel swept up in the tide converging on the balloon. His own instincts would have taken them to the least crowded corner of the park, near the convict barracks, where he could pretend that he was not part of the multitude at all. But the closer they got the more Dowling realised that the pressure was not coming from the people behind but from Isabel, who was determined to stand as close as possible to the balloon when it took off. Before he could do anything to correct the situation, he and Isabel were standing in front of the placard.

'I don't think so,' said Dowling, anticipating the question he could see forming on her lips. 'Your mother…'

'Mama's not here.'

'No, dear, I'm afraid…'

But Isabel was not seeking permission; she was handing him her hat. The half-crown her mother had slipped her as they were leaving meant she could fund her place in history out of her own purse.

'I'm sorry, young lady,' said the tweed-suited man in charge of relieving children of their money. 'Boys only.'

'It says children,' said Isabel, pointing.

'It says children, young lady, but it means boys.' He turned to Dowling. 'Isn't that right, sir? Can't have the little girls taking fright.'

Dowling stared at the faces staring at him. Mortified at this exposure to public scrutiny, he couldn't ignore Isabel's tug on his coat-tails. 'It does say children,' he muttered.

'Indeed it does, sir, but what it means—'

'It should say what it means,' said a square-jawed governess. The point was academic to her since her three charges were boys.

'But it's obvious,' began the tweed-suited official.

A voice shouted over the heads of the crowd. 'It should say what it means.'

'Give the lass her turn,' said another.

The official turned to Swedenborg, as the spokesman for the syndicate. 'I won't answer for the—' Before he could finish his sentence Tobias Smith reached over to Isabel and gallantly scooped her up, provoking an unexpected surge in the crowd that toppled the official and dislodged a wooden peg securing one of the ropes. The jolt upended a sandbag, which knocked over another peg, and in seconds the wicker basket containing Tobias Smith and Isabel Dowling was rising into the sky. Isabel squealed, from surprise more than fear; Tobias Smith rocked back on his heels, and the short fat top-hatted men of the syndicate fell away like skittles as others grabbed hold of the ropes and hauled the basket back to earth.

It was true, technically speaking, as the *Sydney Morning Herald* later reported, that Isabel Dowling at the age of seven was Australia's first female flier.

Tobias Smith's ballooning career took off at twenty-five minutes past three that afternoon when the baker's basket rose over Hyde Park. Five thousand people craned their necks to see him, most wearing gold ribbons, supplied by Swedenborg at cost, to celebrate the colony's glittering aeronautical future.

It was a sunny day with barely a trace of wind. Scoffing at the disapproving looks of his employer, Smith had thrown off his jacket and leant over the rim of the basket in his shirt sleeves.

A hush fell on the crowd as the silk balloon cleared the tops of the trees. A flock of pigeons, annoyed by the intruder, circled noisily in its wake. Boys selling bags of chestnuts stopped shouting and looked up open-mouthed. Marshals in frockcoats and stovepipe hats abandoned their efforts to protect the flowerbeds.

The golden balloon sparkled in the sun like a drop of water while Smith tipped confetti on the upturned heads of the crowd. At a certain point it stopped and hung motionless for several minutes, as if undecided where to go next, before moving off towards the convict barracks.

A cry went up as the gas burner roared into life. It jerked the balloon out of its drift and carried it back into the park, its bulbous shadow rolling like a ball along Cathedral Street.

The balloon travelled so high that Smith was no more than a stick figure who occasionally threw out an arm and waved. If he felt any fear he didn't show it. The truth was he was already bored. A shiny steel clasp kept the balloon tethered to the anchor rope; Smith had half a mind to release it and let the thousand feet of rope fall to earth like a charmed snake sinking back into its basket.

By the time he came down not a flower was left standing. Smith leapt to the ground to receive his acclaim, and was whisked away to steep himself in claret punch. The balloon began to sag. Within an hour it lay on the rose garden, a puddle of spilt silk.

The omnibus men now entered the park, determined to recover the cost of admission by charging double fares for the trip home. They strode around the lawns, cracking their whips and spraying gravel from the footpaths.

Isabel could hardly contain her excitement. She didn't so much walk as hop, snatching up discarded ribbons where they fell. She had forgotten about her statuette and would not have noticed had her father left it behind a tree.

'Wasn't that,' said Isabel as they scrambled aboard a tram, 'wasn't that the most exciting thing you've ever seen in your life?'

Ernest Dowling thought about it. He was forty-three years old with a wife and six daughters and a career in merchant banking. Excitement was not a word he had ever found much use for. It sounded faintly ridiculous, like the figure of the French balloonist and his dog. But if Isabel was asking, was it more exciting than anything else he had seen, or done, or thought of doing, the answer was probably yes. He patted her lightly on the hat. 'I believe so,' he said.

⟨⟩

If it had been up to Miles McGinty, he and his mother would never have left Sydney. They'd have woken at dawn, bolted breakfast and spent the whole day in Hyde Park waiting for the balloon to take off.

Now it was half past five. The train from Parramatta was pulling into Redfern station, having spent two hours stuck outside Strathfield waiting for a body to be removed from the line. The passengers disembarked onto a crowded platform with gold ribbons fluttering from the pillars.

'Oh Miles,' said Eliza, 'I'm sorry.'

Miles, who hadn't opened his mouth since Strathfield, booted an empty tobacco tin onto the tracks. His eyes were moist.

Eliza had tried to temper his earlier excitement with an outing—a train ride to Parramatta and a picnic by the river. Things had started well. In a stables not far from the railway station they had watched a man demonstrate a steam-powered shearing machine. The demonstrator, a hare-lipped Scotsman, managed to scrape half a fleece off a sheep's back before the terrified animal wriggled free. A local grazier, who knew more about sheep but less about mechanics, tried to finish the job but ended up scalding the skin off one arm. Miles, to his mother's surprise, had shown a keen interest in the machine and insisted on looking inside, even persuading the Scotsman to let him watch the gauges. But as they walked down to the river a thunderstorm exploded out of a blue sky. They were soaked to the skin; their lunch was ruined. It was an omen but Eliza failed to see it. The body on the line ruined her plans. Now Miles was inconsolable.

'I'll tell you what, Miles,' said Eliza, sliding an enormous skewer into her hat. 'We'll go and have tea at the Metropole.'

'I don't want any,' said Miles. He slouched the way he often did in public, as if uncomfortable with his height and wanting to appear shorter. His father, he knew, had stood over six feet tall in his socks. Seeing himself reflected in shop windows seemed to remind Miles of his absence. It was not only his own loss that he felt. Miles sensed the anger that, for all his mother's efforts to hide it, welled up in her around the time of his birthday. Every inch he grew seemed to rankle. That was why he enjoyed being in the flies. Up there nobody could tell how tall he was.

'All right. We'll go home.' Home since the end of summer had been a pair of rooms at the Orient, where Eliza's credit would always be good. Wentworth, sailing perilously close to bankruptcy, had ditched Shakespeare for Mother Goose.

A horse-drawn tram stood at the terminus but was in no hurry to leave. A handful of passengers was sitting patiently on the upper deck. The horses had their heads buried in bags of oats. Eliza threw out an arm at an approaching hansom cab. The driver shouted back, 'I'm full, lady,' before leaning back to confer with his fare. 'Where to?' he said, pulling alongside.

'The Orient.'

The driver relayed the information inside then hopped down to open the door. 'Gentleman says he don't mind you coming along.' He paused. 'Full fare, mind.'

They climbed aboard.

'So, young man, did you witness the great balloonist?' The speaker, cocooned in spite of the heat in a heavy Melton overcoat and woollen scarf, edged into the corner to make room for them.

'No, he didn't,' said Eliza, not wanting the subject revived.

'Missed it, did you? That's a shame.' His tone of voice conveyed anything but sympathy. On hearing Eliza's answer he seemed, however, to become bored with the conversation. He turned his head and sat gazing out of the window. It didn't escape her notice that his interest quickened as they trotted through Haymarket, where gaudily dressed women were starting to emerge from the cheap hotels and lodging houses, and install themselves on street corners.

They reached the bottom of Pitt Street and the cab swung left across Circular Quay, past the swaying schooners, towards the Orient Hotel. The man in the Melton overcoat didn't offer to hand them down but sat in his corner with a thin smile on his lips. 'Good night,' he murmured after the driver had shut the door. Eliza paused on the hotel's worn front steps and watched the black hansom cab turn round and head towards Haymarket.

'You'll see the balloon another time,' said Eliza.

Miles was marching up the stairs and didn't hear.

Sydney, which a few weeks earlier had scarcely been aware of Tobias Smith's existence, was all of a sudden proud to claim him as its own. Men and boys elbowed each other to speak to him, thrusting out their hands and slapping him on the back and demanding his autograph. An impromptu committee awarded him a pocket watch inscribed 'Tobias Smith, from the Citizens of Sydney'. Artists begged for the honour of painting his portrait. He was overwhelmed by invitations to balls and parties given by people he had never met.

Swedenborg saw the benefits of keeping his services and offered a raise of a shilling a week. Smith, expecting to be swamped by lucrative offers, was taken aback when none came. The city offered no obvious employment openings for a balloonist. Worse, the syndicate had failed to protect its investment and swatches of silk had been souvenired from the balloon after it landed. The cost of repairs seemed prohibitive. The commercial appeal of a second flight was significantly reduced. Smith, in short, found himself a hero with very little to show for it. He accepted Swedenborg's offer.

Evenings found him at the Castlereagh Club, where he entertained gentlemen from the *Herald* and the *Illustrated News* with slurred tales of his life as a balloonist. He grew side whiskers, plucked his eyebrows and spent more than he could afford on a velvet-collared frockcoat. He affected a knowledge of horses and sheet music.

As the months went by his behaviour became more erratic. He spoke carelessly about friendships with a number of married women. He began to make clumsy requests for money from men he barely knew. He defied Swedenborg's command to remove his whiskers. A year after his flight over Hyde Park, he propositioned the mistress of the editor of the *Australian*. It was his misfortune to be unaware of the intricacies of the marriage. The editor was far more jealous of his mistress than of his wife. Smith's punishment was immediate.

The brokers and bankers who had once been eager to shake hands and buy him drinks now derided him as a vulgar upstart. Gossip columns that had hung on his every word now ignored him. His career in haberdashery ended with a note from Swedenborg informing him that his employment had been terminated 'due to notoriety unbecoming a haberdasher's assistant'.

One blustery day in October 1865 Miles came across Tobias Smith flying a red kite on Coogee beach.

'I'm Miles,' said Miles. He was nine. Eliza sat on a bench on the promenade, clutching the brim of her hat against the breeze. The play she was appearing in—an English farce clumsily uprooted to a drawing room in Randwick—was in imminent danger of closing despite her efforts to save it. The matinees had already been cancelled and Eliza had made the best of a dreary afternoon by walking along the cliffs with Miles. It was she who'd noticed the man in the velvet-collared frockcoat—shabbier now but demonstrably the same garment that was once aped by half the fashionable young men in Sydney. Walking past him, she recognised at once the much-photographed features of the fallen aeronaut.

'Miles, are you?' shouted Smith. The wind blew away the liquor on his breath.

'Mother says you're Mister Smith, the balloonist.'

Smith glanced over his shoulder at the striking-looking woman in the fox-fur coat. He stopped tugging on his line and the kite plummeted to earth. He hadn't shaved for several days. The bottoms of his trousers were ragged. 'I was.'

'Let me try,' said Miles.

'Have you ever flown one?'

'Loads of times.' The lie fell from his lips as easily as those he told his mother on the nights he scrambled unsupervised in the flies, invisible behind the hot lights. Sometimes she thought she saw his shadow moving up and down with the great canvas backdrops. But she could never catch him at it.

Over by the rocks at the south end of the beach a stupendously fat man in a black bathing suit had waded in up to his calves. He stood as still as a statue while the surf frothed between his knees.

'You were there?' asked Smith. 'In the crowd?'

Miles shook his head.

Smith shrugged. He handed over the spindle.

'Were you scared?'

'Balloons are nothing much,' Smith said. 'Anyone can go up in a balloon.'

Miles watched Smith pick the kite up and hold it above his head. But the wind had changed direction. Miles wasn't sure which way to run.

'This is real flying,' said Smith.

'But it's only a toy.'

'One of these could carry a man. If it was big enough.'

Miles raised the spindle and made a half-hearted run along the beach. The kite spiralled behind him bouncing along the sand.

'Give it more line,' said Smith. He was wiping his lips on his sleeve. There was a flask in his hand.

Miles tried again. This time the kite lifted almost vertically into the sky. It fell, then rose again.

'Keep running,' shouted Smith.

The silk kite trembled and danced above Miles's head. He fed out more line, careful not to let it slacken. The power of the wind seemed to pass right through him. Miles kept the kite aloft for nearly an hour, thrilled by its wild spasms and thrashing dives. When it crashed into the wet sand at the water's edge, he turned to find Tobias Smith gone. The fat man in the black bathing suit hadn't moved. The surf was still frothing between his knees. Miles looked along the beach but there was no sign of Smith. Eliza looked up from her book, noticed that Smith was no longer there and stood up.

'I think he was pulling your leg,' said Eliza. They were in a buggy heading down Oxford Street.

'He wasn't,' said Miles, nursing the broken kite on his lap. 'He said a person could fly in one if it was big enough.'

'I don't suppose he said he'd done it.'

'No.'

Eliza was still paying for her mistake in getting Miles back too late to see the balloon. 'Perhaps Mr Smith knows something the rest of us don't,' she said. She didn't believe it but it seemed a harmless enough thing to pretend.

School interested Miles one day and bored him the next. He preferred to loiter by the docks, pestering sailors for stories, making a nuisance of himself among passengers disembarking from Liverpool or New York by begging for their newspapers. Other days he hung around the theatres doing odd jobs, running errands or just watching the actors rehearse.

He mended the kite Tobias Smith had given him. For a fortnight he went every afternoon to fly it from the lawns that sloped from the old government stables to the harbour foreshore. Every time it snagged in a tree he would scramble up and rescue it. Then the line broke and the wind carried it away across the harbour.

But Miles never forgot Smith or his flight over Hyde Park in a balloon. His memory of the event was more vivid for being imagined; assembled from the scraps of gold ribbon he had found scattered around the park the next day and the cheap engravings on sale for a shilling in every second shop window from Circular Quay to Broadway.

Now and then he would go down to the beach at Coogee, cadging a lift or walking if he had to, hoping to catch sight of

Smith. But all he ever saw was the fat man in the black bathing suit, immersed up to his calves, staring out to sea.

⌒

One November evening in 1869 Miles and his mother were walking past the Royal Victoria Theatre when a short muscular man alighted from his buggy. He had a slight limp (one leg was an inch longer than the other) and a wispy moustache stained by years of tobacco smoke. He wore a cream-coloured fez with a frayed tassle like the roots of a shallot, and a dark-green cape. The man paused for a moment before a large, heavily inked poster of a silhouetted figure with his hands outstretched above a levitating child. The words beneath the picture said:

> After his Many Triumphs Abroad,
> BALTHASAR the LEVITATOR Will Demonstrate
> His UNEARTHLY POWERS
> For Five Nights ONLY at the Royal Victoria Theatre.
> Doors Open at Half Past Six.
> LATECOMERS Not Admitted under Any Circumstances.

A murmur passed through the crowd milling on the pavement, indicating that someone had spotted the resemblance between the man and the figure on the poster. Balthasar produced a cheroot from inside his cape and lit it.

His curious complexion (pale and leathery, like antique parchment) and his vaguely oriental looks seemed to indicate exotic origins. His cape trailed a pungent mix of aromas— mothballs, sandalwood, cloves—which suggested a man who had eaten and slept in unfamiliar parts of the world. The twin red circles on the bridge of his nose, evidence of a pair of gold-rimmed spectacles he kept hidden in his cape, implied that he owed his powers to diligent study rather than supernatural gifts. He had blue eyes and cracked lips. It was apparent that he had once laboured for a living. His palms were callused and the little finger on his left hand had been hammered flat on a fence post.

A space had cleared around him. Nobody seemed game to speak to him or shake his hand. He radiated an urbane, perhaps malevolent inscrutability that was all the more impressive for the tattiness of his attire.

It was Saturday night and Eliza was between jobs. Miles, having seen the poster some days earlier, had casually suggested a walk whose true purpose was now revealed. 'Do you want to see him, Miles?' she asked.

Eliza knew what it was to be in the presence of a master magician. Thirteen years earlier, at the very time she fell pregnant with Miles, she'd seen the great Wizard Jacobs perform at the Haymarket Theatre in Melbourne. He was a tall, well-dressed, aristocratic man who was attended on stage by his butler. On the night she saw him Jacobs had jumped a silver-haired ship's captain through a wooden hoop under the delusion that he was a horse. She wondered what tricks Balthasar kept hidden beneath his moth-eaten green cape.

'Wouldn't mind,' Miles said.

On the other side of the road a carriage stopped to disgorge a neatly dressed woman and three of her daughters. They paused to adjust their hats before crossing, the youngest in front and the other two dawdling behind.

There were still tickets left. Eliza was about to hand over six shillings for two seats in the stalls when Miles said, 'Can't we go in the pit?' He always preferred it there, where he could smell the paint on the actors' faces and see them spit as they projected to the private boxes. There was often more excitement in the pit than there was on stage. 'Go on,' he pleaded, until Eliza was forced to give in.

~

The Royal Victoria was not the most comfortable theatre in Sydney. The air inside reeked of horse dung, the legacy of a sell-out production of *The Dog of Montargis* in which the regular cast had been joined by two ponies. Since then it had played host to Shakespeare and Sheridan, among others. Eliza herself had performed there several times. No amount of scrubbing and fumigating had succeeded in expunging the smell. On warm nights like this it hung like a musty blanket over the stage, wafting across the pit and reaching as far as the upper rows of the dress circle, where Louisa Dowling sat with her daughters.

'It's like being in a stables,' complained Rosalind, the eldest, who had been married a year to the nephew of an English admiral: the first of six brilliant marriages that Mrs Dowling had made it her goal to achieve.

'You've never set foot in a stables,' said Isabel, squirming onto the edge of her seat in order to see between the heads of the couple in front.

A dose of flu had excused Mr Dowling from coming, the mere prospect of witnessing a levitation having made his symptoms worse. His duties were confined to obtaining the best seats. This suited his wife and elder daughters but not Isabel. She didn't hide her annoyance, swapping places with each of her sisters in turn before going back to her original seat.

'It's typical of Papa,' she said. 'We'll need a telescope to see what's happening.'

'Nonsense, dear,' said Mrs Dowling. 'We can see perfectly well from here. If Mr Balthasar can do what he claims we'll have an excellent view.'

'I told him we should be in the pit.' Isabel turned to her sisters. 'Didn't I tell him that?'

'I don't think your father could bring himself to enter the pit if he had it all to himself.'

'But he's not here.'

'Oh do shut up, Isabel,' said Helena, who was only eighteen months older but made them all count.

There was no program. Balthasar was prepared to forgo the money he could have earned from them to preserve his mystique. The stage was bare except for a blackboard on which his name was written in elaborate gothic script, and two stools.

Watching him emerge from the wings, muttering to himself as if he'd forgotten something, Isabel was at first profoundly disappointed. She didn't know what a levitator should look like but she was sure he shouldn't be a squat little man in a scruffy cape who gave every impression of being indifferent, not to say oblivious, to the audience. 'Perhaps he's the assistant,' she whispered.

Balthasar waited for silence. He fixed his gaze on what he judged to be an audience's most impressionable spot, half a dozen rows back in the stalls, and said, 'I shall require a body.'

Isabel, instantly forgetting her disappointment, tried to put up her hand but found her mother pinning it in her lap. 'No, darling,' said Louisa. 'I promised your father.' She had promised nothing of the sort but had spotted an acquaintance or two in the private boxes who would not have approved of her allowing one of her daughters to be manipulated in public. An intelligent woman could ignore her husband but not her neighbours.

'But Mama,' said Isabel.

'No, Isabel. I won't let you.'

The question was, by now, academic. A boy had vaulted from the pit and was scrambling up the temporary staircase leading to the stage. 'There you are,' said Louisa, 'someone has volunteered already.' Isabel scowled and perched forwards on her seat.

Balthasar looked him up and down, as though running his eye over a boy was enough to reveal the salient features of his character, and his suitability for levitation. In truth, he was trying to guess his weight.

Miles was not, at first glance, an ideal subject. He was bigger than Balthasar would have liked. Nevertheless, he had raised weightier subjects without mishap and had once floated a sixty-four-year-old woman for seven minutes before her husband called a halt. But these were exceptional cases and carried a risk of failure as well as physical injury. His preferred subject was a child compliant enough to submit to his powers; innocent enough not to recognise the smell of chloroform on his sleeve; and light enough to be lifted by hand if necessary. But now that Miles was on stage it was difficult to send him back.

'Well, young man,' said Balthasar, 'and what's your name?'

Miles told him.

'Speak up, lad. I'm sure everyone would like to hear.'

'Miles McGinty,' he said.

'And where is your mother? Or did you come with your father?'

Miles shrank into his jacket, though to the audience it might have seemed he was merely stooping. Balthasar, after all, was several inches shorter. 'My father's dead,' he said very softly. Balthasar showed no surprise at his answer and seemed, perhaps, mildly annoyed with himself for having asked in the first place.

Eliza stood up, her emerald silk dress shimmering under the houselights. There were admiring murmurs from those who had seen her on stage. Balthasar himself knew her at once and was puzzled to see her among the rabble in the pit. His face, however, betrayed no hint of what he was thinking.

'I must have your consent, madam,' he said. 'The demonstration can't proceed without it.'

Eliza had been taken aback by the speed with which Miles had leapt on stage. She thought it very likely that Balthasar was a trickster and did not want to see him make a fool of Miles. On the other hand she was loath to embarrass her son. 'It is not my consent you need,' she said, 'but my son's.' A ripple of laughter went through the audience.

'Is the lad susceptible?' he asked, frowning.

'He's susceptible to some things,' replied Eliza, 'and not to others.'

'Is he susceptible to the powers of hypnotism? Will he resist?'

'Ask him yourself.'

The levitator had hoped to touch off some nervousness in Miles. Nervous subjects were as a rule more obliging. They succumbed, out of fright, to the soporific tone of his voice or, failing that, to the contents of the blue-stoppered bottle he kept in a pouch under his cape. But Miles was all curiosity, peering about, looking for wires.

Balthasar sat him down on a stool and placed an ebony rod, like a billiard cue, under his left elbow. Then he seated himself on a matching stool and took from his pocket a small piece of polished brass on a chain, which he began to spin by flicking it with the nail of his middle finger.

Miles obeyed his command to gaze at the metal disc. He was conscious of a gravelly voice mumbling away and the smell of tobacco on the levitator's breath. He felt the heat of the gaslights on his cheeks and wished he had pissed before coming in. Miles was drifting off in spite of himself. The spinning yellow disc reminded him of the golden ribbons at Redfern station, which reminded him of Smith and flying his kite on Coogee beach. He was very drowsy now and trying to stifle a yawn. The stage seemed suddenly hotter and brighter, as if someone had turned the gaslights up. Balthasar was still droning on. Miles's eyelids were closing and he tried to open them but the levitator leant towards him, his tar-stained fingers resting on his forehead. A queer sharp odour wafted around his cape, cutting through the smell of horse dung. Miles's nostrils prickled and he was out cold.

Balthasar stood up and removed the stool so that Miles seemed to be sitting on air. Then, as if the boy were a doll, he lifted Miles's legs to one side and straightened them until he was lying horizontally three feet above the stage. His whole body appeared to be supported by the rod under his elbow.

The levitator lit a cheroot and stared at the audience, daring them to believe their eyes while Miles lay there, crossing and uncrossing his ankles, and once trying to turn over before Balthasar gently rolled him back.

A doctor of divinity was invited onto the stage to swing his hand under the body. Two brothers were called down from a box to expose any wires. Meanwhile, Balthasar stood to one side, meeting each gaze he encountered before deflecting it onto the horizontal figure that represented incontrovertible evidence of his unusual powers.

Seeing gravity defied always had the effect of persuading some of the spectators that it didn't really exist, that levitating required no special effort and that flying itself was as easy as falling asleep. Already he saw heads huddled in conversation. A man was shouting at him from the stalls.

In the beginning Balthasar had attempted to convince doubters with a little anecdote, an illustration of aerial cunning analogous to his own. As his skills became more refined the anecdotes grew longer until they blossomed into stories, each delivered poker-faced in the time it took for his cheroot to burn down. Sometimes he told them sitting on his stool; sometimes standing in the semi-darkness at the back of the stage. In big theatres such as this he took advantage of the raked auditorium to wander very slowly along an invisible line an inch or two from the front of the stage, giving the impression (at least to those in the upper seats) that he might at any time step off, or that he was actually gliding above the pit.

'In the early 1600s,' he began, 'there was a Sicilian apothecary called Scarpinato, who lived above his shop near the cemetery of San Giuseppe Jato, a few miles from Palermo.

'Scarpinato was a druggist by trade but fancied himself as an artist. His preparations were famous for their exquisite scents and delicate colours. It was said by his admirers, men as well as women, that a single whiff of his potions could send a person into raptures. The priests disapproved and so did Madam Scarpinato, who hated the sight of all those unmarried women flirting with her husband while he huddled over his scales.

'The apothecary loved nothing better than sitting in his yard watching the songbirds flying among the olive trees. Bit by bit he came round to thinking a man could fly if only he looked hard enough and studied how the birds did it. Scarpinato's genius was noticing how their wings weren't flat but curved. So when he set about making his own wings he chose the most flexible thing he could find, which was whalebone, and pulled it into shape with steel springs. He then covered it with feathers.'

A voice from the pit shouted out, 'How did he get his hands on a whale?'

Balthasar flicked the ash off his cheroot. He did his best to discourage interruptions. 'Scarpinato,' he went on, 'wasn't driven by the desire for money or fame. He simply wished to give his neighbours the chance to experience the playfulness of a bird in flight. He knew nothing about velocity or friction or trajectory. He'd never heard of Galileo.'

'The bloody whale—' the voice interrupted again.

Balthasar answered curtly, 'It was beached.'

'Get much oil out of it?'

It was apparent the heckler had some experience of whaling. Balthasar adjusted his cape and tried to ignore him.

'Go on, how much oil did they get? No point in taking the bone without the blubber.'

Others shouted him down and the levitator was allowed to continue.

'The site Scarpinato chose for his flight,' said Balthasar, 'was a sugar mill high in the hills of western Sicily. He longed to show off his wings but only when he could prove they worked.

'The mill tower was three storeys high. It had stood since the middle ages but no-one had lived in it for years. A little stream flowed down the stony hillside, watering the garden and the nearby orchard, although the race that once powered the wheel was dry.'

The levitator pursed his lips and expelled a puff of smoke. Miles remained motionless, a disembodied spirit eavesdropping on his tale, while Eliza looked on anxiously.

'There was no glass in the windows,' he went on, 'and Scarpinato, by clambering onto a ledge, was able to launch himself from a height of nearly thirty feet. The courtyard was strewn with broken flasks and the stone flags glistened with syrup trodden in over the centuries. A sickly sweetness hung in the air. The crickets screamed and the birds lurched about as if they were drunk.

'From the ledge Scarpinato could see into a valley which swept down to the town of Partinico and the sea. Further up the hillside was the village of Montalepre with its faded terracotta roofs and bare stone walls. The mill, tucked into a broad ravine fringed with olive trees, was well hidden to guard against bandits who roamed the hills, robbing and murdering unwary travellers.

'Scarpinato claimed to have glided a hundred and fifty feet before landing in the middle of an almond grove. The only proof he could offer was a broken spar in his wing and some damage to one of the almond trees. A shepherd found him bathing his feet in the stream and took him back to Montalepre.

'Returning to Palermo, the apothecary found that rumours of his feat had preceded him. People made jokes at his expense. Children wore paper wings on their backs. Madam Scarpinato was enraged by the mocking looks from people who had once queued for hours outside her husband's door. She didn't believe his story for a minute and blamed his hallucinations on working with the windows shut.

'At first Scarpinato's four daughters sided with their mother but then they changed their minds, chastised her for her lack of faith and insisted their father would fly again to prove his doubters wrong.'

The Dowling girls looked at each other accusingly. Isabel opened her mouth to shout but was silenced by her mother.

'This,' said Balthasar, 'was further than Scarpinato had intended to go. His leap from the sugar mill, far from convincing him of the beautiful possibility of flight, had persuaded him that his whalebone wings would never work. He owed his life to his voluminous pleated sleeves which had filled with air and broken his fall.

'A great melancholy descended on him. He rarely got out of bed before lunch, and he handed out his preparations in unwashed bottles. The vision that had inspired him was dead. He drifted sadly towards the day nominated for the demonstration.

'Exactly a month after his unseen flight from the mill a crowd of Sicilian notables, church dignitaries, shepherds and merchants gathered to watch Pietro Scarpinato jump from the mill tower and break his neck on the shiny flags below. His curved wings were buried with him in the churchyard of Saint Jude, the patron saint of lost and desperate causes.'

The levitator dropped the stub of his cheroot and ground it under his heel. The aim of his story was not to win applause but to focus the minds of his audience on the floating figure. His preferred response was awed silence but Sydney rarely gave him that. He heard instead the relieved babble of theatregoers convinced they had got their money's worth. It was a familiar response and suited him well enough, though he always hoped for something more dramatic.

Eliza kept her admiration to herself. She knew what it was to hold an audience enthralled. She had seen charlatans do their hocus-pocus on blackened stages, hiding their apparatus behind screens and smoke. But Balthasar, she thought, was the real thing: a master magician.

At last he replaced the stool and clapped his hands twice. Miles sank like a butterfly settling on a leaf. When he stood up the floor felt very strange. Applause rolled towards them. Isabel did not join in. She hadn't wanted the story to end. And seeing the boy wavering in the lights reminded her that she could have been the one on stage. Her mother put an arm around her. 'Didn't you enjoy it, darling?'

Isabel scowled and said, 'We were too far away.'

Miles's mind was a blank. Between sitting down and getting up he remembered nothing. As he walked down the steps he felt a strange dizziness. It was as if he'd been floating not three feet above the ground but a thousand. Somewhere in the back of his mind was a story about an apothecary. Did he hear it or dream it?

The demonstration had lasted barely half an hour. Balthasar had learnt not to linger after the applause began to fade. He understood the delicacy of belief and knew better than to expose his artistry to a second look. He hobbled off the stage and never, ever came back.

'Well?' said Eliza. 'Aren't you going to tell me what it felt like?'
Miles was striding across Bathurst Street. Eliza struggled to keep
up.

'Weird,' said Miles. 'As if I was dreaming. There was an odd
smell. Then I woke up.'

Eliza pulled him towards her. 'What sort of smell?'

'Sort of…sickly.'

It was almost nine o'clock in the evening. There wasn't much
traffic in the city, only the odd buggy clattering down the middle
of George Street. They stopped at a tap room in Kent Street.
Beneath a large advertisement for Horatio's Boomerang Brandy,
Miles sawed his way through a fat rump steak. His body from the
shoulders down felt somehow detached, as if he was feeding
someone else's hunger. He ate like a horse.

The public bar of the Orient Hotel was crowded as usual.
The smell of beer and sawdust came out to meet them. They
walked up the staircase, taking care not to trip over the broken
carpet rods. Halfway up, Eliza caught a whiff of something
exotic, tobacco smoke with a hint of cloves. Miles smelt it too.
There was no window above the stairs. A veil of smoke hung
around the gaslight. A third of the way along the corridor was a
wicker chair. Sitting on the chair, casually perusing the racing
columns of the *Sydney Morning Herald*, was a short muscular man
in a collarless grey shirt and flannel trousers.

'Pardon me,' he said, lowering the newspaper but in no
hurry to stand up. 'I took the liberty of anticipating you.'

'I can see that,' said Eliza. She recognised him now as the
levitator.

'I could have waited, only…'

'Only you couldn't wait.'

'Exactly.' He folded the paper and slipped it inside his shirt. Removing the cheroot from his lips, he shaved the ash from the tip and extinguished it with a wet finger. Up close he was not a bad-looking man, though his teeth were not in the best of shape. It was impossible to guess his age; the years had left a sort of patina on him, though his eyes were bright. 'Hello Miles,' he said, 'I hope you're none the worse for your levitation.'

'No,' answered Miles. He remembered the question about his father and didn't want to hear it repeated.

'I hadn't expected to find you in such a place,' said Balthasar, glancing at the worn carpet and shabby wallpaper. It was twenty years since a carpet had been replaced or a door repainted. Some of the wallpaper was original.

It occurred to Eliza to ask how he had found them but she let it pass. Her whereabouts, after all, were known to any reader of the gossip columns. Her devotion to the Orient Hotel was a source of amusement to her peers, most of whom favoured more luxurious accommodation.

'We like it,' she said, 'don't we, Miles?'

'Why are you here?' asked Miles.

'A business-like question, lad,' smiled Balthasar, 'and one worth answering.'

The levitator stood up slowly and, with a slight shuffle of his eyebrows, indicated that the conversation he had in mind was not one to be had on a public landing. As if to confirm the shrewdness of his judgment, a door opened, revealing the swaddled head of an elderly woman whom Eliza had seen once or twice eating kidneys in the private dining-room downstairs. Seeing a stranger in the corridor, the old woman pulled her head in and bolted the door.

'Do you make a habit,' asked Eliza, 'of following people home?'

The levitator pointed out that he had, in fact, preceded them. 'I hope you'll forgive me,' he said.

The stalemate could have persisted indefinitely: Eliza refusing to open her door without knowing why he had come and Balthasar refusing to discuss the matter on the landing. Miles was about to intervene when his mother took out her key and shooed the two of them inside.

Miles's room adjoined hers. The connecting door was open. Balthasar glanced in as he walked past, as though he expected to see some evidence for a conclusion he had already reached.

Accepting the offer of a chair, he began to explain the reason for his visit. Levitation, he remarked, was a delicate business; it required rare powers of co-operation and concentration, to say nothing of the etheric matter. This, he said, was a substance far more refined and subtle than the rarest of physical matter. To those, like himself, equipped to see it, it appeared as a thin band of light and energy surrounding the body. It was commonly silvery-blue or grey but in Miles's case it was reddish, and exceptionally brilliant. In order to produce a levitation, one had to energise the etheric matter (he didn't go into details), whereupon the subject would rise into the air and remain suspended until the trance was broken. For reasons he didn't wish to go into, he had been sceptical about lifting Miles. But Miles was an unusually amenable subject. The boy levitated as if he was born to it. It was as much as he could do to stop him flying away. Balthasar knew it. And so, he was certain, did Miles.

For a while the three of them looked at each other without speaking. Balthasar was an expert bullshitter, a master of the art.

He knew just how long to spin out a story. 'Your son, Mrs McGinty,' he said at last, 'has a very saleable talent.'

'Miles is only thirteen,' said Eliza.

'No doubt you performed at a younger age.'

'What about his lessons?'

Balthasar had the flinty scorn of the autodidact for the inside of a schoolroom. 'He seems bright enough, Mrs McGinty. I dare say it would be nothing to impart to him the odd bit of algebra if he showed an interest.'

Miles pulled a face.

'What exactly are you proposing, Mr'—she hesitated—'what *is* your name?'

The levitator scratched some grit out of his fingernails. He had gone under the name Balthasar for so long that he hardly remembered any other. He used it for bank accounts and doctors' prescriptions. But his parents were Poles; the name he was born with was Wolunsky and he grudgingly owned up to it.

'Wolunsky?' said Eliza.

'Zbigniew.'

'Zbigniew Wolunsky?' Each syllable was perfect. Eliza had not given her life to the stage for nothing.

Wolunsky massaged the knuckles of his left hand, which were swollen from arthritis. It was many years since he had heard his name spoken so beautifully. He could not conceal the effect it had on him. A suggestion of a tear formed in one eye. 'As I was saying, it is not every day…that one…stumbles upon such a gift. It would be a pity to waste it.'

Eliza fiddled for a moment or two with a loose thread in her dress, allowing the levitator to pull himself together.

'Let's say what I have in mind is a pooling of talents. Your own, Mrs McGinty, are of course celebrated. Mine have a certain notoriety. I have an idea that Miles here may upstage us both.'

Miles kept his thoughts to himself. The levitation had left him with the oddest sensation, as if parts of him had floated away and were only just returning. He had pins and needles in his fingers and the soles of his feet itched. He could hardly wait to do it again.

'As it happens,' Eliza said at last, 'we were thinking of a move.'

Wolunsky was an attentive reader of newspapers and had gathered that Eliza was not currently engaged.

Sydney was already uncomfortably humid. 'I suppose there are worse ways of spending a summer,' she said.

'Undoubtedly,' Wolunsky agreed.

Eliza looked at him suspiciously. 'I won't have him drugged.'

'If you are referring to chloroform,' said Wolunsky, glancing at Miles, 'it is merely a precaution for…unresponsive subjects. In your son's case I'm convinced it won't be necessary.'

'What do you think, Miles?'

Miles dug his fingers into the armchair. 'Wouldn't mind,' he said.

⁓

They left Sydney a fortnight later in a mud-spattered coach with Eliza's leather trunk strapped to the roof. Their first stop was at Richmond, where Miles floated for half an hour before the members of the Total Abstinence Society. A week later at Lithgow, they repeated the feat at the request of the New South

Wales Early Closing Association. In Oberon, a hundred and
twenty lapsed and current members of the Band of Hope Society
watched in silence as Wolunsky raised Miles above his head and
sat down to read a newspaper.

Months went by. They travelled through the fierce heat of
summer and the vicious cold of winter, saw the sky darkened by
locusts and watched gum trees exploding with cockatoos. They
were in Bathurst when the Macquarie River burst its banks,
stranding them for a week, and were chased by a bushfire (started,
at a guess, by a carelessly extinguished cheroot) on the road to
Cowra. In Grenfell a scholar from the Paris polytechnique and
an Irish professor from Trinity College had to be prised apart
when a fight erupted over the metaphysical implications of what
they had seen.

At forty-eight, Eliza found her new role unexpectedly
congenial. Thirty years of her life had been spent on the stage.
She had grown so used to the crust of powder on her cheeks that
the sensation of wind and rain on her skin was exhilarating. Now
she gave impromptu renditions of Shakespeare to temperance
women and timber cutters, sometimes in the same tent. She saw
the country as she had never seen it before, discovering the fierce
beauty in a blackened hillside or a paddock of flooded gums.
When they travelled by mail coach she often sat alongside the
driver, clinging onto her hat as they hurtled down hills and
splashed through fords.

Miles didn't say much. He was suspicious of Wolunsky and
his intentions towards his mother. But the boy was smart with his
hands, ingenious with a hammer and saw, a resourceful impro-
viser—skills he had picked up from mechanics and scenery men.
When their coach overturned in the Cudgegong River, it was

Miles who righted it. He was proud of his usefulness. Six months after setting out from Sydney, he made Wolunsky an elevated boot to ease his limp.

The levitator was overjoyed. He stared at the boot, built up with a three-quarter-inch block of yellow box filed down at both ends.

'It'll take a bit of getting used to,' said Miles. 'It's not light.'

'Lighter than having a dead leg hanging from your hip.' Wolunsky sat down and put on the boot. 'You're a clever bugger, lad, you know that?'

This was a handsome compliment from the levitator, who didn't give them out lightly and mistrusted those who did. Miles shrugged in a pretence of indifference. The truth was he looked up to him. Though reluctant at first, he now submitted willingly to the lessons that Wolunsky gave him on mornings when he was not otherwise engaged. The levitator seemed to know everything. He carried around with him a supply of books in his native Polish, though he professed not to be able to speak the language. Over the years he added to his collection by buying from Polish immigrants, of whom there appeared to be many.

'You'd be amazed,' said Wolunsky. 'Wherever there's a scent of gold, the Poles are never far behind. Like the celestials, lad. We've got a nose for it.' He tapped his own which, unlike the rest of him, was long and angular.

Eliza watched from a distance as the levitator put his weight on the stunted leg and took a few clumsy steps. She too had grown fond of him. She had seen Miles standing up straighter in his presence; had heard him, with a cup of cocoa in his hand, become almost garrulous.

'I owe the lad a debt, Mrs McGinty,' he shouted, lumbering towards her on his new boot. 'Your son has made me whole.'

⌒

Without his stage garb, Wolunsky looked much like anyone else: a bow-legged fellow who'd seen too much of the sun. He spoke quietly and bit his nails. His shirts could have used an iron. There was nothing about him to put another bloke on his guard.

Stories followed him around the country, macabre tales that might or might not have been true. Men recalled seeing him walk out of pubs leaving his companions suspended several inches above the ground, or with a mug of ale halfway to their lips. There were incidents, mostly in small towns along the Murray River, in which (it was said) people found themselves inexplicably transported from one room to another, or conveyed across the river without their knowledge. A publican in Corowa, on the New South Wales side, put it about that he had started pulling a pint for a man he'd never seen before—short, sly, taciturn: it had the ring of truth—and the next thing he knew he was sitting in a paddock five miles away in Rutherglen.

These tales grew in the telling, like stories of nuggets lifted out of the dirt by picnickers, or dried-up creek beds glittering with alluvial gold after a week of rain. They often came in pairs, one trying to outdo the other.

When they reached Wolunsky's ears, as they always did sooner or later, he offered no comment, merely raising his eyebrows and looking away.

In Victoria the gold rush was over but in New South Wales the fever raged. The roads were crowded with clairvoyants, water-diviners, hypnotists, cabbalists and pea-and-thimble men worn out from the heat and dust of the diggings. They trudged home from the goldfields yellow-skinned and dog-tired, angling for a feed in return for some shoddy fortune-telling or jiggery-pokery with a weighted dice.

Some carried Bibles, which they flung open at the 'dust of gold' in Job, or the 'city of gold like clear glass' in Revelations, gazing into the gum-strewn hills as if they were the promised land.

There was a man in Narromine who claimed he could turn stones into bread and sand into nuggets. Another in Tumut swore he was immune from fire and could toss himself off mountain peaks without a scratch. There were men who could talk to mules and others who conversed with frogs.

At the Gunnedah Hotel, a one-legged prospector reckoned he could make himself disappear by drinking a pint of gin and brought out a mirror to prove it. An old bloke on the verandah swore he'd met Moses on the fields at Kiandra.

Wolunsky listened to these stories and smiled. He could tell a clever stunt when he heard one.

⌒

Four years passed. Miles became cockier, more audacious, less willing to play the role that Wolunsky had created for him. He became so adept at emptying his thoughts before the spinning brass disc that he stopped closing his eyes, to the annoyance of Wolunsky, who found it hard to concentrate with the boy staring at him. Once Miles was airborne, the levitator could move him about the room with the barest touch of his little finger. Miles became convinced that he was moving about on his own. He performed meretricious tricks—balancing a glass of water on his forehead, signing his name on the ceiling—and on one occasion startled Wolunsky by floating through an open window.

The levitator would clump away on his elevated boot to consult his books. 'Temperature, Miles. That's what it is. Temperature's the answer. Your etheric matter evaporates when the temperature gets up. I reckon that would explain it. We'll have to keep an eye on that in future.' Once he suggested tethering him by the ankle to keep him from drifting off.

Miles stared doubtfully at the thin leather belt by which the levitator wanted to restrain him.

'It'd just be a precaution,' said Wolunsky, 'in case...' He didn't finish the sentence. He couldn't bring himself to admit to any doubts about his own powers.

'In case I float away and never come down?'

'Shh, lad. We don't want to worry your mother.'

Miles was seventeen. He had continued to grow but seemed less conscious of his height than before. At his age the lack of a father needed less explaining. He wore a collarless shirt and moleskin trousers and liked to go about barefoot. The sun had darkened his olive skin; his cheekbones had grown sharper, his neck longer. Something about his stance suggested a heron poised over a pool.

The beginnings of a moustache had appeared in time to impress the young women who, by virtue of his height, mistook him for someone older. He'd fallen briefly in love with the daughter of an actress, a girl who never addressed him except through her mother and who left unopened his awkward offerings of flowers and pencil sketches. He was more confused than hurt; the girl's mother had had her eye on him first.

They spent Christmas Day 1873 in Yass, where Miles entertained an audience of charcoal burners by hovering for a few
minutes above a bed of hot coals.

Wolunsky could no longer be sure that his protege would
remain suspended for twenty minutes or half an hour. Sometimes
Miles would start moving almost at once, heading for the windows
which the levitator had been careful to shut. Other times he
showed signs of waking up before Wolunsky was ready; his eyes
would open, occasionally he yawned. It was impossible to know
how much of it was deliberate. The levitator had to be more
careful with his stories, knowing they might be cut off at a
moment's notice.

'There was a Dutchman,' he began, 'a nutmeg trader, name
of Meerschaum.'

The audience was a gathering of graziers and graziers' wives
in Tumut. They had watched prospectors trudging up into the
mountains in search of gold, standing knee-deep in the freezing
Tumut River from dawn to dusk and emerging, if they were lucky,
with a handful of yellow specks to put in an empty tobacco tin.
They would come down half starved, or not come down at all.
This lot knew all about obsessions.

'Meerschaum built himself a pair of wings made of iron and
goose feathers attached to a tight-fitting leather girdle. He was a
big, clumsy man, the son of a flour miller. As a boy he'd lugged
huge sacks of wheat on his shoulders. He had thick biceps and
flapped his wings for an hour each morning to build up his
strength. Flying, he was certain, would be easy but he didn't trust
himself to land safely.'

Wolunsky glanced over his shoulder to make sure that Miles
hadn't done anything unexpected.

'When did this happen?' inquired a grazier's wife in the front row.

'1668,' replied Wolunsky.

'He knew Rembrandt, then?'

'Pardon?'

'Rembrandt, the painter. He was Dutch. They probably knew each other.' The woman's husband nodded his support, though he had never heard of Rembrandt and was keen to hear how the story turned out.

'Painted sheep, didn't he?' asked a grazier several rows back.

'Horses,' said another.

Wolunsky waited until the interruptions ceased. 'Meerschaum,' he went on, 'spanned a nearby river with pontoons covered with layers of straw mattresses to break his fall. On the appointed day he leapt from the top of a wooden tower. One of his wings snapped and instead of gliding he plummetted onto the mattresses.'

'There's a bloody moral there,' one of the audience remarked gruffly.

'But the pontoons,' said Wolunsky, 'had filled with water and the force of Meerschaum's landing made them capsize. The straw mattresses became saturated and sank on top of him. Meerschaum, hampered by his iron wings and unable to wriggle out of his girdle, drowned.

'The big crowd watching from the banks did nothing to save him, thinking it was a stunt to whip up business for the spice trade. Public notices printed a week later expressed astonishment that the nutmeg seller didn't surface after his accident. The mayor blamed Meerschaum's grieving widow for encouraging her husband to the act that caused his death.'

Miles had begun to tilt. His feet were rising slowly towards the ceiling. The blood was rushing to his head. Wolunsky reached hastily for an ending.

'A patent on the sinking pontoons,' he said, 'which Meerschaum had had the foresight to take out in his wife's name, made her an immense fortune when the design was used in reclaiming land for the port of Rotterdam.'

'Who'd have bloody thought it,' mumbled a voice at the side.

But the first grazier's wife wasn't satisfied. 'Well, did he or didn't he?'

'Did he what?' asked Wolunsky, gripping Miles's feet and wrestling him back to the horizontal.

'Know Rembrandt?'

The audience now waited for an answer. But Wolunsky was too distracted to offer one. Miles was rising again. It was as much as Wolunsky could do to hold him down.

At this moment Eliza got up from her seat and walked slowly to the front. Even in such a ramshackle place, she knew how to make an entrance. 'Indeed he did,' she said, her rich voice echoing off the walls. 'Mister Meerschaum was his brother-in-law, younger brother of the first wife who died. Rembrandt painted him once, dressed up in his wings and leather girdle. But the portrait was lost in a fire. Dozens of canvases were destroyed, including'—she gazed unhurriedly about the audience—'all his sheep pictures, and a good many of his horses. Of course his wife's death had left him heartbroken. The spark had gone out of him. From that day on he painted no-one but himself. The portraits grew darker and darker until there was nothing but black. Then one day he put down his palette and never returned to it.'

By now Miles had been brought back to earth. Eliza turned round to see Wolunsky snap him out of his trance. She indulged herself in a long actorly pause. 'Rembrandt,' she said at last, 'died in poverty, poor man, with only his mistress and son to mourn him. He left nothing but some old clothes and a handful of paint-brushes.'

They spent summer in the Riverina before returning to Wagga Wagga, where they relaxed for a month in furnished lodgings above a bank. A nagging uncertainty over his powers was beginning to take its toll on Wolunsky. He suffered cruel aches and pains, a catarrh that often kept him awake until the small hours. He would clutch Eliza's arm as they sat in the coach, his swollen fingers gripping her like a claw. A paunch began to hang over his trousers, though it seemed to Eliza that he survived on nothing but tea and vegetables, obscurely metabolised by the smoke he was forever sucking into his lungs.

As they travelled north they found themselves caught among the hordes streaming towards the goldfields at Mudgee and Gulgong, where a Mr Saunders had sparked the rush by digging up fourteen ounces of gold in two hours. Now Gulgong had a population of 20,000 in mud and weatherboard huts, with a pub on every corner.

When there were no coaches to be had or carriages to be hired they travelled in carts. Wolunsky would hole up for days on end, huddled over his books, looking for the answers to questions he could hardly bring himself to ask.

Sometimes Miles wandered off, leaving it to Wolunsky and

his mother to contrive some entertainment for the dwindling audiences who still came to see them. Not that Eliza would ever consent to be lifted in public—Wolunsky had attempted it once, behind locked doors, and found her unsuitable—but she was happy to assist in demonstrations using well-behaved children and sometimes an obedient cattle dog.

One morning, as they ate breakfast in a Bathurst hotel, Miles came across an article in a discarded copy of the *Central Plains Herald* dated 1 April 1874:

A SAMARITAN REWARDED

Mr Tobias Smith the balloonist, whose disgrace was as complete as the triumph that preceded it, and whose dissipation long condemned him to oblivion, is reported to be aviating once more thanks to the kindness of Mr William Mayfair, the renowned entertainer, who found Mr Smith in a state of great extremity beside the Windsor toll road and nursed him back to health. In return for his Samaritan's deed, Mr Smith has resumed his ballooning career as a member of Mr Mayfair's famous Travelling Circus, which has been performing to appreciative crowds in the MEROO RIVER valley and may be seen in the coming weeks in the towns of RYLSTONE, MUDGEE and GULGONG before launching itself upon SYDNEY.

'I'm going to see him,' said Miles, pushing away his empty plate.

'See whom, Miles?' said Eliza.

'Smith.'

'Not the balloonist?' said Wolunsky, reaching for the

newspaper. He read the item and shook his head. 'I thought the poor bloke had done away with himself.'

'Well, he hasn't,' said Miles. There was now a sharp edge to every conversation between them, though it hadn't stopped Miles making a new pair of gusset boots for Wolunsky, complete with elevated soles, when the others wore out. Miles was bored. The limitless blue sky he looked up at every day seemed to mock Wolunsky's tent-show magic.

'It's a gimmick, lad,' said the levitator.

'And you'd know all about them.'

Wolunsky ignored this remark. 'In a few years it'll be submarines. Then electric railways.'

Eliza, too, had never forgotten the sight of Smith on Coogee beach, though what she remembered was the tatty frockcoat and frayed trousers. She had seen others ruined by their own success. She could not find it in her heart to condemn them. Looking at the newspaper, she felt a strange obligation to witness the resurrection of Tobias Smith.

'I think we should all go,' she said. 'I'm sure Mr Smith will be glad of our support.'

'I have nothing against Smith,' Wolunsky insisted. 'It's just—'

'That's settled then,' said Eliza, calling for the bill.

William Mayfair's Travelling Circus, featuring Miss Camilla the rope-walker, Signor Monteverdi's acrobatic elephants and Mr Smith the world-famous balloonist, had been on the road all summer. Gold had been found up and down the Meroo River and Mayfair, ever alert to the generosity of lonely prospectors, had struck it rich in the ragged hamlets that sprang up along the river and its tributaries. Now, with the weather turning colder and Monteverdi's elephants becoming fractious, he looked forward to fleecing the graziers in Mudgee before dragging his troupe over the Blue Mountains for their annual assault on Sydney.

It had rained during the night. The elephants' feed was sodden and they were refusing to eat. There had been last-minute arguments over unpaid wages. At midday Miss Camilla emerged from her trailer and told the crowd huddled under umbrellas on Mudgee racecourse that her hamstrings would not allow a performance that day.

Half the crowd promptly demanded their money back. The rest waited patiently in the mud for a promised announcement at one o'clock. At two o'clock Mayfair mounted a small dais. 'Despite a headache,' he began, before correcting himself. 'Despite a severe headache, brought on by the inclement weather, Mr Smith has agreed to be hoisted at four.'

At ten minutes to five, Smith descended the steps of his trailer. It was clear to anyone who cared to look that he'd been drinking. His bloodshot eyes rolled lazily in their sockets. He didn't notice the drizzle as he stumbled towards the balloon. He looked puzzled by the sight of so many umbrellas and managed a pallid smile as he climbed into his basket, his black coat-tails flapping behind him.

On the far side of the racecourse, Signor Monteverdi was parading the larger of his elephants, a giant bull called Hector, around the track. A handful of small children squatted by the starter's gate, pelting the animal with sticks. Hector, dressed for the occasion with a red velvet choker around his wrinkled neck, glanced sideways with a look of infinite disdain before emptying his bowels in the middle of the straight.

It was almost dark before the balloon began to climb, watched by a crowd that included Miles, his mother and Wolunsky.

The conditions were far from ideal. An electrical storm filled the sky with corkscrew currents. The air fizzed as though it might catch fire.

The golden sphere that once soared gracefully over Hyde Park—Mayfair had salvaged it along with its pilot—was now patched with squares of black cloth. It wallowed above the treetops like a great jellyfish, trailing ropes and dripping clods of mud.

Smith gazed from his basket with a look of grim resignation, his cadaverous features exaggerated by the gas-fired shadows that leapt across his face. Now and then he turned his back and suckled on a flask of cheap brandy.

'Personally,' Wolunsky began, but Miles hadn't come to listen to what the levitator had to say, personally or not. For years he'd dreamed of watching Tobias Smith ascend in a balloon. Now he'd seen it he wished he hadn't. He'd come to see a hero and found a drunk. The balloon wheezed overhead. Smith could hardly keep his own balance. Miles saw him turn and vomit into the basket.

Monteverdi turned Hector around and began to goad him with fistfuls of hay towards a barricaded enclosure where he, another elephant and three horses would spend the night, each tethered to an iron stake which any one of them could have uprooted with ease. Hector was taking his time but was content to play along, unlike Monteverdi, who resented the trouble he was being put to and made no effort to disguise his irritation.

The cause of this frustration was the knowledge that Miss Camilla, despite her tender hamstrings, was sitting in her trailer in her nightgown. Monteverdi knew from experience that timing was all-important with her (as it had been with her predecessor, Madam Lucille the ball-gazer) and that her welcome would cool with every minute she was kept waiting. He knew as well that the offence would not be quickly forgotten and that he would spend several days in purgatory before he was forgiven. But what was the point of arguing with an elephant? There was no better nature he could appeal to; no punishment he could threaten. All he could do was keep stuffing hay in its whiskery trunk.

Hector lumbered massively towards the open gate and stopped. Something was annoying him. He looked askance at Monteverdi, as if demanding an explanation, before lowering his head and pushing over the barricade, which crumpled like a paper lantern. The men dropped the ropes they were holding and ran.

Oblivious to the commotion, Smith chose this moment to fire his burner. With nothing securing it, the balloon shot upwards.

Miles watched in silence as the balloon reached five hundred feet, a thousand, rising like a bubble in a glass cylinder. It was found the next day three miles away, draped over the branches of a huge ironbark in which Tobias Smith hung upside down, with his neck broken, like a bat caught in telegraph wires.

⁀

Smith died in the rain and was buried in it. His broken body was carried in a brass-handled coffin on the back of one of Signor

Monteverdi's elephants, with Mayfair and Miss Camilla on the other. The hotels and shops along Market Street drew their blinds out of respect. Eliza and Miles watched from the upstairs verandah of the Woolpack Hotel as the cortege plodded up the hill towards the cemetery, where an Anglican minister prayed for sun under a leaky umbrella.

That evening, in the hotel's public bar, Mayfair proceeded to spend what money he had, and the little he was able to borrow, celebrating the short life and sudden death of Tobias Smith the balloonist. He saw Miles on his own in the corner, his mother and Wolunsky having retired—separately, and in opposite directions—to bed.

'Young man,' he called out.

Miles didn't move. He had his own reasons for regretting what had happened. He'd had a vision and now it was lost.

Mayfair pushed back his stool, gathered up his glass and a half-full bottle of whisky, and carried them over to where Miles was sitting. There were now only half a dozen drinkers left in the bar and none who hadn't already been subjected to the entrepreneur's maudlin reminiscences.

'You knew him, sir, no, of course not. Our Mr Smith, godblessim, not the most talkative of men, no friends…bit of a loner, you'd have to say.'

Miles hadn't said a word but Mayfair seemed capable of keeping the conversation going on his own.

'Great man,' he went on, 'brave man, never seen him shrink from a challenge by God, not many of us you can say that about. Found him in a ditch as good as dead and…you said you knew him? Too bad. Too bad. Newspapers called him a balloonist but he was nothing of the sort. Scoffed at 'em, he did. All I could do to talk him into it. No future in 'em, he said, anyone can go up in a balloon. Need an engine if we're ever going to fly.' He finished his drink and poured another. 'Kites, kites were his thing. A man could fly across Sydney Harbour with a kite. No good without money, that's what I told him. Wish I'd never'—he drew back for a better look—'he never mentioned you, lad. I'd have remembered if he had. What was the name again?'

Miles told him.

Mayfair screwed up his face—'McGinty? McGinty?'—then continued with his monologue. 'Only three of us there at the last. Monteverdi, Camilla, myself. Newspapers killed him. Don't suppose he felt a thing. Been drinking, lad. Should never have let him go up but he insisted on it. Reckless, that was the trouble with him. Set his heart on flying. Not balloons, no, never trusted 'em. Swedenborg put him up for it. Ribbon-seller. Call him an evangelist—Smith that is, never lost the faith. We'll all be flying one day, he said. Always scheming and dreaming. Page after page of bloody flying machines.' The entrepreneur fumbled in his pocket and slapped a leatherbound notebook on the table. Then, from his other pocket, he produced a silver watch engraved with the words 'Tobias Smith, from the Citizens of Sydney' and an odd-looking pair of castanets which he seemed to have carved himself. Miles opened the notebook. The handwriting was so chaotic he thought at first it was written in code.

'Never saw him without these,' said Mayfair. 'No use to him now, godblessim. Pass 'em on, he said, if the worst ever happens. Never will, I said, trust me. Only it did, didn't it?' He stared at the things on the table. 'Pass 'em on to who? No friends, poor devil, only three of us there at the last. Monteverdi, Camilla, myself. Put 'em in the coffin, says Monteverdi. But that ain't passing 'em on, is it?' He looked up at Miles, who was slowly turning over the pages of the notebook. 'You take 'em, lad. Spoke about you, I'm sure. Bit of a loner, Smith, kept himself to himself. What was your name again?' He got up, tipped back the last of his drink and started unsteadily for the door. 'Sorry you didn't come sooner,' he said. He paused for a long while, as if trying to work out who he'd been talking to, then murmured, 'Damn sorry.'

The Dowlings' hall was long and narrow, made narrower and longer by having the walls painted dark plum. It reminded Isabel of the inside of a coffin.

Though a great hoarder of some things (especially sons-in-law), Mrs Dowling was indifferent about others. The house was stuffed with furniture but almost bare of ornaments, which she liked to dismiss as 'dust-gatherers'. Those the family did possess were often given a prominence they hardly deserved. Consequently there was room on the hall mantelpiece for a nondescript brass statuette entitled '*Le balloniste et son chien*'. Mr Dowling had learnt to live with it without ever banishing from his mind the suspicion that it represented some vulgar gallic joke that none of them understood.

The sight of the statuette as he returned from work one evening reminded Dowling of something he had read while riding home on the omnibus. He found Isabel in the sitting room, playing a game of backgammon against herself. Since the engagement of his fifth daughter, Helena, to the heir of a rubber fortune, Dowling had become mildly concerned over the future of his youngest, who would soon be eighteen years old. Not that he shared the determination of his wife to see Isabel engaged before she turned twenty. He was disappointed by his daughters' husbands. None of them encouraged him to expect diverting conversation over brandy and cigars as he grew old and lame. He didn't care to speculate on what sort of a husband Isabel might attract but he knew it wasn't conducive to a young woman's prospects to be playing backgammon alone.

'Hello, my dear,' he said, standing in the doorway.

Isabel was scowling. The part of her that wasn't winning seemed to resent the part that was. 'Hello, Papa,' she said, not looking up.

Her occasional peevishness still alarmed him. She could still turn on a shocking temper. He wasn't sure if he should come in. 'I thought this would interest you,' he said, indicating a small obituary hidden among the classified advertisements.

Isabel's expression brightened. The interruption, she decided, was welcome after all. She knocked the counters off their positions and read the newspaper over his shoulder.

> We are sad to report the accidental death of Mr Tobias Smith, the balloonist, whose deeds once featured prominently in these pages. Mr Smith, after a long period of infirmity, had lately returned to the dangerous occupation that made him famous. We are assured that his courage was evident to the last. Mr Smith was interred in the cemetery at Mudgee, attended by those who counted themselves friends.

'Poor man,' said Isabel, remembering how Smith had reached out and swept her gallantly into his basket. 'Fate wasn't kind to him.'

Mr Dowling furrowed his brow, as he always did at the mention of fate. He believed that a man made his own fate. He, for one, left very little to chance. But he was aware that some men made poor decisions and suffered because of them. The world, he knew, was not a gentle place. He remembered Smith as a balloonist, not as a drunk.

'He deserved better,' said Isabel.

Isabel Dowling had plenty of admirers. There was nothing surprising about that. An unmarried girl—pale, fashionable, well-off—was bound to have suitors swarming around her.

Sydney was full of young men on the make, insurance salesmen, tobacco importers, speculators in gold and wool, articled youths of various persuasions, all eager to attach themselves to the daughter of a decent family living in a mansion in Stanmore.

The house was big but not portentous, ornate but not vulgar, set at the top of a sloping lawn that offered an uninterrupted view of the railway line to Parramatta. The roots of an immense fig tree had undermined the south-east corner and a jagged crack was working its way towards a hexagonal bay window in the sitting room.

Isabel had received her first proposal a few weeks before her fifteenth birthday. Even then, she was easily mistaken for eighteen. She dressed beyond her years and never discussed her age. It was a premature but plausible offer by a man only seven years her senior who took his refusal badly and was sent off at once by his parents to make his fortune in Singapore.

In the three years since, she had had several more, all less attractive than the first. Her suitors had a habit of turning up unannounced, bearing bunches of flowers they couldn't name, enthusing about plays they couldn't remember. At first Isabel enjoyed playing them off against each other. She began by asking how they would solve the problem of the fig tree, which at its current rate of growth would in twenty or thirty years have advanced several inches into the sitting room. Those who recommended poisoning, ringbarking or otherwise destroying the tree soon realised their prospects were ruined. Isabel's view was that the tree had been there first and if anything needed altering it was the house. Her father didn't share her opinion.

As each pretender fell by the wayside, others appeared to take their place. Sydney produced a year-round supply of tolerably good-looking, adequately prosperous but vapid young men who had nothing better to do with their Sunday afternoons than dress up in stiff collars and flatter Isabel's mother.

Isabel could bear it for a few months at a time before she had to take refuge at the house of her maternal uncle, Dr John Galbraith, in Emu Plains, where the subject of marriage was never raised and she could help herself to whisky. The houses were a mere thirty-five miles apart but they inhabited separate worlds.

For now, however, she was in Sydney and had to make the best of it. At seventeen and three-quarters she was no longer interested in the fig tree. Suitors who came prepared to discuss horticulture were disabused.

'The fig tree?' she said, glancing at the cracked mortar. 'I've no idea. I expect someone will do something about it sooner or later.'

A man named Edward Ramsay was walking a few steps behind. They had met at a party. He was boring and handsome with ambitions in the retail trade. Isabel's mother had taken a shine to him and invited him to lunch.

'Gorgeous weather, isn't it?' said Isabel. 'I don't think I've seen a cloud all month.'

'Very nice,' Ramsay agreed. He spent most of his time in his office and rarely looked out of the window.

'April's always been my favourite month.'

Ramsay positioned himself so that it would have been no trouble for Isabel to put her arm through his. 'Tell me, Edward,' she said, flitting off towards the roses, 'do you have an interest in politics?'

'Er…'

'Free trade, that sort of thing.'

'Oh, yes.' He caught a glimpse of Mrs Dowling smiling at him from an upstairs window.

'Where do you stand on the woman question?'

Ramsay buried his face in a white rose. 'These smell pretty,' he said.

'Rubbish,' said Isabel. 'They have no scent at all. But the red ones aren't bad.' She bent down to confirm her opinion. 'Women, Edward—I suppose you have a position? Everyone must have a position. My father's position is that we must be properly dressed. My mother's is that we must be married.' She could see that Ramsay didn't have the faintest idea what she was talking about. 'Equality, Edward. Should we have it or shouldn't we?'

'Of course.'

'Of course what?'

'Of course you should'—he puckered up and sniffed a red rose—'if you want it.'

Ramsay had never read John Stuart Mill's *The Subjection of Women*, a battered copy of which Isabel had bought for sixpence in a book stall. It had sat ever since beside her bed, waiting to be opened. 'Naturally we want it,' she said. 'Why wouldn't we?'

Ramsay shrugged. He couldn't imagine why a woman would want it, especially one as young as Isabel. 'I really don't know,' he said.

Mrs Dowling, when inviting him to lunch, had primed him with conversational subjects that might interest Isabel if they happened to find themselves alone together. With that in mind he'd gone to the expense of sitting through more than half of a dull play at the Prince of Wales Theatre. He couldn't remember enough of the plot to introduce it himself but was confident of being able to hold his own if the topic came up. He took a monogrammed handkerchief from his pocket and coyly blew his nose on it.

'You don't deny we are just as clever as the men?' said Isabel. 'Or cleverer?'

Ramsay didn't respond except by folding his handkerchief and putting it back in his pocket. Isabel hadn't noticed before how meticulous he was in his personal habits. She caught him looking at a spot of mud on his trouser cuff.

Her mother, sensing that things were not progressing as she had intended, opened one of the french doors from the sitting room and came across the lawn to meet them.

'Edward,' she said, 'what a very elegant suit. I'll have to get the name of your tailor for Mr Dowling. Isabel's sister is to be married soon and his morning suit is falling to pieces.' She fingered the sleeve of his jacket. 'Then it will be Isabel's turn.'

Ramsay opened his mouth to supply the name but before he could speak Isabel cut in. 'Edward is convinced both sexes are the same.'

Louisa Dowling's face collapsed and took some effort reassembling. Neither she nor Mr Dowling ever took Isabel's political opinions seriously. As her parents they felt it their duty to listen. But Mrs Dowling didn't expect others to be so complaisant. High on her list of requirements for her last son-in-law was that he would stop Isabel making a fool of herself. 'Really, dear?' she said.

Ramsay looked embarrassed. His cheeks turned a shade of pink that almost matched his tie.

'How very…progressive of you,' Louisa said.

'I'm not at all sure, Mama,' said Isabel, choosing this moment to put her hand through Ramsay's arm, 'that he wouldn't vote for us if he got the chance.'

A pained smile tugged at Ramsay's face. He was not in love with Isabel though he had imagined he soon would be. He couldn't guess at Isabel's feelings but hoped they would in time fall in with his own. He thought Mrs Dowling was very taken with him and hoped he'd made a good impression on her husband. In short he'd have been happy, before this moment, to make Isabel his wife. But the prospect of discussing politics over breakfast was enough to put him off his kippers.

Renewing his interest in the roses, Ramsay withdrew Isabel's arm from his own. It slipped out easily.

'Lovely, aren't they,' said Mrs Dowling. She shot a long-suffering frown at Isabel, then suggested Ramsay might like to join her husband in a sherry. She did not expect to see him again.

Isabel and her father were standing on the front porch. It was half past three and there was already a chill in the air. Dowling cast a quizzical gaze over the rose beds, as if noticing them for the first time. 'Didn't seem quite your sort, Isabel.'

He couldn't have said what Isabel's sort was, or even what 'sorts' were on offer, but he'd heard the word spoken by two girls on an omnibus and had been waiting for an opportunity to use it.

'He was Mama's sort,' said Isabel. 'I thought you'd have guessed that.'

Dowling contemplated a stroll in the garden. 'Is there any prospect, do you think, that your mother's sort and yours might ever coincide?' He paused. 'I only ask out of curiosity, my dear. Of course it's none of my business. Your mother and I have no wish to interfere.'

'Mama does nothing but interfere,' Isabel corrected him.

Miles had been tempted to leave them all on the table: Tobias Smith's notebook, his silver watch, the castanets. Smith had let him down; he didn't need these mementoes to remind him. For a couple of days he didn't even look at them. Then curiosity got the better of him. He opened the notebook. The pages were crammed with words and figures, columns of untidy sums, rough pencil sketches and elaborate diagrams in Indian ink. It wasn't just idle doodling; each page was numbered, each diagram labelled. These were not the maunderings of a drunk but the dreams of an aeronaut, the work of a a visionary.

Smith had spent his last years hunched over books about

flight, designing models he would never build, conceiving theories he would never test. After Swedenborg had thrown him out, he found work in a carpenter's factory, turning table legs. He imagined himself learning the skills to build a flying machine. It was self-pity that drove him to drink. He knew he had ruined his hopes. A man with the shakes couldn't work a lathe. Mayfair had tried to save him but Smith didn't want to be saved.

Miles kept his find to himself. He didn't know what else to do. For a week or two, things went on as before. Miles continued to upstage his mentor, though in a perfunctory way that convinced Eliza he was up to something. She had seen him poring over the leatherbound notebook and asked what he was reading. 'Nothing,' he said.

She glimpsed the sketches and guessed what they were. She caught him sitting in his clothes at three o'clock in the morning in a hotel in Hill End, carving a propeller from a stick of ironbark.

They were in Sofala where a few dozen prospectors clung to their stakes, though most of the gold had long been dug out and melted into bars. It was May 1874. The weather had turned sharply colder. Wolunsky's knuckles had swollen up like roots of ginger.

The sun shone white in a vast blue sky. Dusk fell suddenly. Twenty-odd prospectors gathered in the only building big enough to hold them: a rotting weatherboard shell that had once been the Methodist church. 'Well, lad,' murmured Wolunsky, 'shall we get started?'

'I s'pose,' said Miles.

'Something simple to begin with, eh? And then we'll see what happens.' After all the roads they'd travelled together, all the halls they'd filled, all the audiences they'd bamboozled, Wolunsky still liked to give the impression that he had a few tricks up his sleeve, a rabbit he could pull from under his cape if the need arose. And perhaps he believed it, though the routine was by now so familiar to both of them that they could do it in their sleep.

As the room fell silent, a rooster crowed somewhere in the darkness. Hearing it, Wolunsky turned an artful smile on the shovel-bearded prospectors, who glowered back at him unmoved.

Miles couldn't stifle a yawn as Wolunsky straightened him on his stool and positioned the rods under his elbows. He'd been up most of the night, reading Smith's notebook. He glanced at his mother. Their eyes met only for an instant but it was enough to tell Eliza that something was different.

Wolunsky sat down and took the brass disc and chain from his pocket. The surface of the disc had become tarnished and he took a few moments to polish it. Miles stared at him as he rubbed. He watched the levitator's bulging eyes, the whites yellow and veined like the glaze on an old jug. He saw the tufts of stubble on his chin, the moth holes in his cape. This was Balthasar, the pot-bellied master of magic.

The disc began to spin. The audience leaned closer. Wolunsky cleared his throat and began pouring out a toneless stream of mumbo-jumbo. The rooster crowed again. Miles shut his eyes but his heart wasn't in it. He thought of Wolunsky with a red comb wobbling on his head and feathers on his throat.

He showed no more inclination to levitate than the rough-hewn benches on which the shovel-bearded prospectors sat and scowled. Wolunsky's voice grew louder and more desperate. Miles, however, didn't move.

It wasn't in Wolunsky's nature to lose his temper. When angry or disappointed or embarrassed, he simply withdrew his presence, sometimes so completely that he might as well have been invisible. The fact that he was still there in person compounded the discomfort of his companions.

Miles had intended to apologise, not for what he'd done but for the way in which he'd done it. He expected to do it over breakfast and to be silently rebuked for the rest of the morning. But Wolunsky's chair remained empty. When Eliza went to knock on his door, she found his room deserted. His bed hadn't been slept in. His cape and fez lay on the floor with the gusseted boots Miles had given him.

It was nine o'clock in the morning. Miles and his mother stood on the rickety verandah of the Sofala Hotel, staring at the unearthly landscape of bare stumps and bark huts and mullock heaps. 'You made a fool of him,' said Eliza. 'After all he's done for you.'

'You mean after all I've done for him.'

Eliza picked up the moth-eaten cape and laid it softly on the levitator's bed. 'Mr Wolunsky was levitating people long before you came along.'

'Then he doesn't need me.'

'Of course he doesn't,' said Eliza, though she knew it wasn't true. Wolunsky was no longer the man who had cornered them on the landing of the Orient Hotel. The tension had gone out of him. It pained her to see him warming his sore knuckles in front of the fire. She said quietly, 'You humiliated him.'

'I've had enough,' said Miles. 'I'm going to Sydney.'

Eliza had been waiting for this. 'It's that balloonist, isn't it?' she said. 'He's put some foolish idea in your head.'

'What if it was in my head first? What if it's always been in my head?'

'We should never have gone to Mudgee.'

'I'd have gone without you.'

Eliza sat down on a straight-backed chair—the same chair, to judge by the ash ground into the verandah, that Wolunsky had been sitting on before he vanished. 'Don't underestimate Mr Wolunsky,' she said.

'Bugger Mr Wolunsky,' replied Miles. 'Don't underestimate me.'

At half past three that afternoon Miles hitched a ride on a cart bound for Capertree on the Sydney road. He spent the night in a hay shed. The next day the mail coach from Mudgee clattered out of the fog with Miles on board. He had with him a winter coat and twenty-two guineas which Eliza had counted out of her cashbox into his hand. In the pocket of his coat was Tobias Smith's notebook.

The other passengers, two sisters and a widowed lawyer from Gulgong, sat avoiding each other's gaze while the coachman sang a maudlin song. The girls smiled as Miles climbed aboard and he smiled back.

At the crest of a steep hill the coachman jumped down and requested help in attaching a log to a short chain he wanted to hang from the back of the coach in case the vehicle ran away. Seeing the Gulgong lawyer pretending to be asleep, Miles winked at the sisters and hopped out, making more fuss of the job than it deserved and clambering back in time for the lawyer to open his eyes and ask why they weren't moving.

The driver was an old hand; he knew every bend and pothole in the road. The horses trod cautiously at first, speeding up as they reached the bottom and having to be reined in for the log to be removed. After that it was Ben Bullen with its glittering snow cap and beyond it the dark saddles and sunlit spurs of the Blue Mountains.

They spent the night at Blackheath and drove on at first light, only without the lawyer. Miles and the sisters were now on first-name terms. A dense white fog swirled through the valleys, pooling in hollows where the coachman could scarcely see beyond the swinging tails of his horses.

Miles accepted the offer of a corner of the sisters' blanket and the three sat with their knees touching as the sun began to unmask the red sandstone cliffs. A second night had given him time to think. He didn't regret leaving; he was certain of that at least. Even his mother had seen the inevitability of it. But Wolunsky's disappearance had left things unresolved between them. It was as if Miles had stolen away with something that didn't belong to him: stories he only half remembered that had to be returned, if not to Wolunksy then to someone else.

'There was an Umbrian nobleman,' he said, 'called Giovanni di Torto.'

Miles didn't know how the sisters would react. It was one of the first tales he'd ever heard Wolunsky tell. He wasn't even sure how it ended. If they so much as glanced at each other, or looked in their laps, he'd stop.

It was too cold to play cards. 'Go on,' said Abigail, the younger of the sisters.

'He was a lean, handsome bloke,' said Miles, 'with a long

nose and moustache, told a good yarn, had a feel for horses. He put all his gifts to use galloping around the country trying to rustle up money for an idea that would make Umbria the centre of the scientific world.

'Many of the nobles coughed up large sums to claim a share of his new invention. It would be the marvel of the age, he said, something to put Galileo's telescope in the shade. Dazzled by his charisma, they didn't question him too closely on how he planned to build it—'

'Build what?' asked Abigail.

Miles realised he'd forgotten the point of the story. He felt the blood rushing to his cheeks. 'Wings,' he said. 'Made out of iron hoops stretched with goatskin.'

'Did he make them himself?'

'Of course not,' said Rebecca, her sister, 'he was a nobleman. He'd have got someone to build them for him, wouldn't he, Miles?'

'They were made by the local blacksmith,' said Miles.

'Did he have a name?'

'Alfredo.'

'Let him get on with it,' said Rebecca.

'The blacksmith—'

'Alfredo,' Abigail reminded him.

'Exactly. Well, he insisted on double-bracing all the major joints, and using the finest kid leather and the most delicate stitching. The price went up and up and it began to look as if the wings would never be finished. Finally di Torto ran out of patience. He dismissed Alfredo the blacksmith and had one of his stablehands finish the job instead. This bloke substituted cowhide for goatskin and used rough stitching better suited to a laundry sack. He had them finished in a week.

'Di Torto took one look at the wings and knew they weren't up to it. The cowhide was too coarse; the forging was shoddy. But the money men were getting restless. He went to Alfredo on his hands and knees but the blacksmith was sulking and refused to lift a finger.

'On the sixteenth of February 1650 di Torto pulled on a bronze helmet, splashed himself with rose water and jumped to his death from a tower in Perugia, watched by his wife, three children and half a dozen household servants. The iron wings were sturdier than he'd imagined. While his own body was battered beyond recognition, his wings survived the crash with barely a dent.

'His two sons, Antonio and Gianluca, now vowed to succeed where di Torto had failed. Their father's widow, who was remarried within a year, was powerless to stop them. Her new husband set about breaking up the estate and selling the land to the same neighbours who'd paid for di Torto's wings. The brothers were too caught up in their own rivalry to care about what happened to their father's property. In any case they'd inherited his belief that the wings, once perfected, would be worth a fortune. But here's the rub—'

'The what?' asked Rebecca.

'The rub,' repeated Miles. He'd heard the phrase so many times that he thought Rebecca was having him on. 'You know, from *Hamlet*.'

Both girls eyed him dubiously. '*Hamlet*?' they chorused.

Miles was nearing the end of his story. He didn't want to lose the thread now. He could tell, however, that they weren't satisfied. 'To sleep,' he said, 'perchance to dream.'

'Sorry?' said Abigail.

Miles hesitated. He didn't want any more interruptions. 'The old man,' he said, 'had been a real enthusiast, a dreamer who let his pride get the better of him. But his sons were merely rivals; they knew nothing about aeronautics and cared less. It never dawned on them that they were outdoing each other to repeat their father's fatal mistake.

'Fifteen years to the day after his leap, they both climbed the same tower, elbowing each other up the narrow spiral staircase while a team of servants followed a few steps behind with their wings.

'The weather was perfect, not a cloud in the sky. A stiff breeze blew from the south-west. A huge crowd filled the square. Half wore yellow in support of Gianluca and the other half wore green for Antonio. The servants cursed and spat at each other from the ramparts. Di Torto's widow, wearing one ribbon on each wrist, sat with her new husband in a pavilion a hundred yards from the base of the tower. She couldn't bear to watch.

'Neither son was prepared to give the other the honour of jumping first, so both jumped at once. They hit the ground together and died of ruptured spleens, abusing each other to the last for having soiled their father's memory.

'On their mother's orders, the wings were carried off and thrown in the Tiber, along with di Torto's whole library, his diaries and notebooks, and everything else that reminded her of the obsession that had robbed her of a husband and two sons.'

'Is it true?' asked Rebecca.

'Of course it is,' said Miles. 'Every word of it. You can still visit the tower in Assisi where it happened.'

The sisters looked at each other. Abigail corrected him. 'You said Perugia.'

At Katoomba they were joined by a man in a heavy Melton overcoat and black woollen scarf. Something about him seemed familiar to Miles, though he couldn't say what. The stranger nestled at once, like a dog in a basket, into the corner of the seat.

His arrival was a disappointment to the others, who were looking forward to the prospect of travelling on alone. In his presence their conversation became awkward. He left no doubt that he was listening to every word.

The newcomer remained silent as far as Parramatta, though his mouth opened from time to time as if to comment on the view, only to close again without speaking. The sisters played cards, glancing from time to time at Miles.

At Parramatta the man loosened the black scarf around his neck in order to remark that the Parramatta River, though broad in places, was less broad than he remembered it. The sisters ignored him and carried on with their cards. His observation hung in the air between them until Miles turned away from the window and said, 'The rivers are all running low. It's been a dry summer.'

The stranger considered this observation for a while. 'A meteorologist, are you?' he said.

Miles had never heard the word before. 'Am I?'

'A student of the atmosphere. A watcher of winds. A forecaster of weather.'

'I didn't forecast it.'

'But you evinced some familiarity with the subject.'

Miles stared at the stranger, who had a queer waxy complexion, as though he'd been dipped in tallow. He wished he could recall where he'd seen him. He guessed by the look of the leather holdall he'd seen slung on the roof that the stranger was going all the way to Sydney. He fished Smith's notebook out of his pocket.

'It is an interesting subject, the weather,' said the newcomer. 'In Africa locusts fly upside down in anticipation of rain. Their antennae detect the rise in atmospheric pressure.'

Miles pretended to be reading. The stranger, however, was determined now to engage him in conversation. He repeated his former statement word for word, adding, 'Is that not extraordinary?'

'Is it true,' said Miles, looking up from his book, 'that their organs turn back to front in sympathy? That they take food at the rear and expel it at the mouth?'

'I have not heard that, young man. It may be true but I have not heard it. I shall enter it in my journal. An educated man should always keep a journal. It is a useful receptacle for the knowledge he does not yet possess but would profit from acquiring. Mine, you will note, is not large.' He pulled out a little black book and scribbled a few lines. 'Have you ever, by chance, seen a whirlwind?' he asked.

Miles began to suspect that he was a schoolteacher. 'Several,' he answered.

'Then you have seen the loose matter sucked into its vortex? Dust and leaves and whatnot?'

'Yes.'

'Pressure, young man. The differential causes material to be sucked from the higher pressure to the lower. The rotation is faster on the perimeter than at the centre; consequently the force is directed inwards. I'll wager you have never seen anything ejected from a whirlwind.'

The sisters looked up from their cards. The shadow of a grin passed across Miles's face. 'Only once,' he said.

'Oh?' replied the stranger.

'I once saw a foal spat out of a whirlwind,' said Miles. 'Near Gundagai. It flew half a furlong before landing in a pond.'

The stranger weighed up this information without comment. They continued two or three miles before he spoke. '"Dropped" is the more accurate word,' he said. 'The word "spat", besides being a vulgarity, implies propulsion, which is impossible, meteorologically speaking. Articles have been seen to fall when a storm abates. Otherwise the sky would be full of roof shingles. Are you certain it was a foal?' He didn't wait for an answer. 'The ancient Greeks,' he said, 'were convinced of the existence of a winged horse. According to the myth, Pegasus sprang from the blood of the slain Medusa. I doubt you are familiar with the poet Ovid. You do not strike me as a man versed in the classics.'

'I have read *Mother Goose*,' said Miles.

'Have you indeed? And did you admire its structure? Its faithful adherence to the principles of Aristotelean drama?'

'It made me laugh.'

'I have no doubt it did, young man.'

The coach was slowing down. A bullock cart had shed its load of apples and a crowd had gathered. The driver, between abusing his bullock and kicking the cart, was swearing at passers-by to keep their hands off. The stranger seemed to recoil at the sight of the crowd, and sank deeper into his seat.

For an hour they travelled in silence. Miles flicked through Smith's notebook until he arrived at a page of drawings: sketches of windmill blades, ships' screws, flying seed pods, frangipani petals. Smith had been obsessed for a time with what he called the 'wind screw'. He was convinced it could be used to propel a machine through the air.

For some time the stranger had been watching Miles out of the corner of his eye. He could no longer contain his curiosity. 'What, may I ask, is that?'

'A book.'

'I can see that. What sort of book? Not a published one, I gather. A diary, perhaps? Do I take it the author is a child?'

'It was written by Tobias Smith.'

'The balloonist?'

'You've heard of him?'

'I remember some notoriety attached to the name. Is that still his vocation?'

'He died. In an accident.'

'Human beings,' the stranger observed darkly, 'were not meant to fly.'

'And who decided that?' asked Miles.

'Nobody decided it. It was determined. By Nature. And by God.'

'I've never heard a sermon that said it.'

'One does not take one's theology from sermons, young man. One goes to the horse's mouth, by which I mean the holy scriptures.'

'The world's full of machines,' said Miles.

'Indeed it is. I once shared this very conveyance with a gentleman—a physician, I seem to recall, from Emu Plains—who collected them, as one might collect Greek amphora or suits of armour. It was his contention that some individual—an Italian or German most likely—would sooner or later invent a flying machine, not to mention a diving machine and a computing machine and sundry other machines of no value to anyone but himself.' He paused here to remind himself of a joke. 'I remember asking him if he foresaw the day when a dying man would entrust himself to a surgical machine.'

'And he said yes?'

A look of annoyance came over the stranger. 'I don't recall his answer.'

'Someone invented the sewing machine,' said Miles. 'What's to stop someone else inventing a flying machine?'

'Only the absolute certainty that it will never fly.'

'Tobias Smith flew. Five thousand people saw him.'

'I was not among them,' said the stranger.

'Here,' said Miles, reaching into his pocket, 'they gave him a watch. It says, "From the Citizens of Sydney".'

The stranger held out his hand and made a great show of inspecting it.

As the coach trundled down the slope to Broadway the man fastened his collar and tightened the woollen scarf around his throat. The coachman pulled up just before the Newtown road. He opened the door and said, 'Your stop, Mr Windsor.'

Windsor stood by the road as the coach continued down Broadway towards the city. It was only later that Miles realised he had taken off with Tobias Smith's silver watch.

It was many years since Titus Windsor had lived in Sydney, though he'd made regular visits since. An awkward incident had forced him to leave the grammar school and find work as a teacher of divinity in a parish school in Katoomba. The place was far beneath his talents but insular enough to be careless about what happened outside its walls.

On several previous trips to Sydney Windsor had considered

paying a visit to the family of his sister's husband's cousin. He had even drafted letters with the aim of soliciting an invitation. None had ever been sent. A chance comment by his sister at Christmas had reminded him of their existence. He posted a letter, received a lukewarm reply, and was now deciding whether to walk the three miles or so to Stanmore or splash out on a hansom cab.

He had brought little luggage. His black leather bag contained a minimum of clothes, a shaving razor and a few books. The road was mostly flat; there was no prospect of rain. He decided to walk.

At a quarter to seven he arrived in magnanimously good spirits at the door of the red-brick mansion overlooking the railway line.

'Good evening,' he said, dropping his holdall at his feet and extending a pale hand to the attractive middle-aged woman who opened the door.

It wasn't Mrs Dowling's habit to shake the hands of strangers. Mistaking him for a salesman, she began to retreat, but this enticed Windsor over the threshold. 'You don't recognise me,' he said.

'No,' said Louisa.

'Titus,' said Windsor.

The name rang no bells.

'I wrote to you,' he said.

'Yes, of course…Mrs Redmyre.'

'My sister.'

Louisa smiled uncertainly. 'Er…you'd better come in.'

Windsor stood where he was, as if expecting someone to take his luggage. 'I appear to have arrived in time for dinner,' he said. 'Of course you were expecting me.'

'Tomorrow,' said Louisa, 'but never mind.' She heard footsteps coming down the stairs and turned to see Isabel, who decided she had forgotten something and scampered back without a word.

'My daughter Isabel,' said Mrs Dowling.

'Indeed,' replied Windsor, following his nose towards the dining room, where a bow-legged, short-tempered servant was already putting the first serving dishes on the warmer.

'Matilda,' said Mrs Dowling, 'there will be one more for dinner.'

The servant shot an aggrieved look at Windsor and went off to fetch another plate.

After weighing up the fitness of each of the six chairs placed around the long mahogany table, Windsor settled on the one that by dint of the silver cigar cutter on its left clearly belonged to Ernest Dowling. Windsor himself didn't smoke, had never smoked, no doubt never would. So he had no need of the cigar cutter which he ordered to be passed down the table to its owner, who accepted it in stunned silence.

As the nearest thing in the room to his blood relative, Mrs Dowling braced herself to be the object of Windsor's conversation. But the schoolmaster believed himself to have a special bond with youth. He pulled a series of alarming smiles at the two daughters still living under their parents' roof. 'Titus Windsor, my dears,' he said. 'I am a teacher of divinity. You may call me Uncle Titus.'

His eye was particularly taken by Isabel who, besides being the prettier, was also closer. She wore a bright yellow dress that stopped a few inches below her knees and was frayed at the hem. Instead of shoes she wore a pair of red Chinese slippers. Her fair hair spilled over her shoulders in a way that suggested she didn't make a great fuss of brushing it.

It was Windsor's habit to dominate a conversation, to conduct it by himself if necessary; at the very least to decide the subject, monitor the contributions, and interrupt as and when he chose.

'You know, my dear Isabel,' he said as he shovelled potatoes onto his plate, 'I shared the coach with three young persons of a similar age to yourself. I was entirely in my element.' The tip of his tongue flickered behind his teeth in anticipation of the roast leg of lamb that Mr Dowling was carving.

'Really?' Isabel replied without enthusiasm.

'It was my intention to improvise for them a short dissertation on the subject of the weather.'

'I hope they were grateful.'

'I have no doubt they would have been. My experience of young people is that they are, for the most part, instinctively willing to learn from those with more knowledge of the world than themselves.' He hoped for some endorsement of his finding but none came.

'Did you change your mind?' Louisa asked politely.

'Certainly not, Mrs Dowling. I never change my mind once it is made up. It gives a bad example. In my profession one must always be conscious of examples.'

This statement seemed to Mr Dowling to make good sense. He grunted his assent.

'No,' continued Windsor, 'I fully meant to carry out my intention and would have done so had a more pressing subject not intervened between us.'

'More pressing,' asked Isabel, 'than the weather?'

'It is not a frivolous matter,' her mother remonstrated.

'Indeed, Mrs Dowling,' said Windsor. 'I think Isabel's interest confirms that.' He helped himself to five large slices of lamb, licked his lips, then took a sixth.

'The subject, you will be surprised to hear, was ballooning.'

Isabel didn't look nearly as surprised as he had hoped. In fact she looked bored, though the truth was she was eager to hear and determined not to show it.

Mrs Dowling gestured to Matilda to relieve him of the lamb, which seemed to be hampering him in his remarks.

'The young person—I did not ask his name—was of the opinion that ballooning was a respectable ambition for the common man.'

Mr Dowling, though shrewd enough in his own line of business, rarely trusted himself to contribute to casual conversation. He was uncomfortable with banalities and didn't enjoy sharing his opinions with strangers. It was not uncommon for him to sit for an hour or more at a dinner table without opening his mouth except to eat. On the scant occasions when he did volunteer a comment, it was usually at his wife's urging. Glancing at her now, he saw a look that said it was his duty to save them all from the monologue that was forming on Windsor's lips. What Louisa had in mind was some mundane but masculine question (was there a telegraph station in Katoomba?) that would put Windsor off his stride and allow them all to eat their lamb in peace.

Dowling grasped the need to speak but was at a loss for something to say. In the end he took his cue from Windsor. 'Isabel,' he said, 'once ascended in a balloon.'

Miles's first thought was to head straight for the Orient Hotel. He'd always been friendly with John Fogerty and could expect a warm welcome there. But his appearance was bound to invite questions about his mother and Wolunsky which he had no desire to answer. So he got out as they approached Hyde Park. The sisters waved as he left. They hoped to see him, they said. They didn't say when.

He took a room in a nearby boarding house squeezed between a butcher and an umbrella shop. Sydney had changed, but not much. The horse-drawn trams that used to clatter down Pitt Street were gone. There was talk of steam trams with double-decker cars but for now the streets were clogged with horse omnibuses and hansom cabs. Old buildings had fallen down, or been knocked over, and new ones were going up. By midday the air stank of beer and smoke and tanning shops.

The city was full of familiar faces: shopkeepers and barrow men, lamp-lighters, liveried doormen hopping like sparrows outside the smart hotels in George Street. Theatre bills showed many of the same old names, actors who'd shared the stage with his mother. Mr Delillo was reborn as a great tragedian at the Prince of Wales. Wentworth, the impresario, was preparing to tour his new *Mother Goose* to Newcastle. One morning Miles stood outside the Prince of Wales and fancied he could hear the hiss of the gaslights inside.

'It ain't like it used to be, Miles,' said a voice behind him. 'It is Miles, in'tit?' It was an old woman speaking. 'You haven't forgotten me, have you?'

It was Mrs Gwilym, who had once played Ophelia to Eliza's Hamlet. She was bent almost double but walked without a stick and carried a string bag containing a loaf of bread and a few onions.

'Of course not,' said Miles. Shaking her hand didn't seem right. He bent down to kiss her on the cheek and caught her, as she intended, on the lips.

'You was always a bright one, Miles. Why are you here?' She was as brusque as ever. 'Your Mr Balthasar still on the scene, is he?'

'His name's Wolunsky.'

Mrs Gwilym seemed affronted that she hadn't known this. 'Queer sort, from what I heard.'

Miles didn't say anything, but he didn't have to. She guessed what had happened. 'Flown the nest, eh? My littluns was all gone by fifteen. Visit me sometimes, they do.' She stopped to scrape something off her shoe. 'So what are you doing?'

Miles shrugged. 'This and that,' he said

'Where are you staying?' She didn't wait for his answer. 'Carry these for me, will you? We'll have 'em for supper.'

So Miles ended up sleeping in the attic of a tiny terraced house in East Sydney with a front door opening onto the pavement and a window upstairs from which he could see the tops of the fig trees in Hyde Park. He shared the space with dozens of costumes which hung from the roof beams like kippers in a smokehouse. There was no pension for retired actresses but Mrs Gwilym lived comfortably doing what she called 'private commands' in the coffee houses and tea rooms in the city.

She dragged out of Miles the story of his break with Wolunsky and his mother. She listened without comment. When he'd finished, she said, 'You must write.'

Miles frowned.

'She'll want to know you aren't dead in a ditch,' said Mrs Gwilym.

Within a day or two it became clear that Miles didn't know what to do with himself. The old woman put her foot down. 'Vic's after a flyman,' she said. It was a few minutes past six in the morning and she was standing in the attic in her nightgown. She had a cake of soap in her hand and a threadbare towel.

'Vic who?' asked Miles, still half asleep. He'd been dreaming of the sisters from Mudgee.

'Royal Victoria. You haven't forgotten it, I hope. Their flyman took off a week ago and no-one's laid eyes on him since. You know the job. Keep the sky from falling in. Bit of painting and set-building when it's wanted. You could do it with your eyes shut.'

His eyes were barely open as it was.

'Briggs is the manager,' she said, handing him the towel and soap.

'Briggs,' repeated Miles.

'Wife died last year. Nine children. He drinks.'

Miles went down there three hours later and was hired on the spot. Seasoned flymen were hard to come by and Miles had been climbing the ropes since he was four. He was also handy with a saw and paintbrush. Briggs, an affable, beery man, had been a great admirer of Eliza and upped Miles's wages by half a crown a week to show it.

Staring up at the great vaulted roof, with its painted moon and stars, Miles remembered the night Wolunsky had levitated him for the first time. He imagined Eliza railing and weeping to the boxes. Some part of each of them lingered here.

He sat down one night to write to his mother and Wolunsky. He didn't know where she was but he knew she never drove through Blackheath without stopping at Mrs Sullivan's Tea House. A postcard there would reach her sooner or later. But what would he say? He could hardly explain to them what he couldn't explain to himself: that he'd always dreamed of flying and that Smith's drunken visions would show him how. 'Arrived safely,' he wrote. 'Old faces everywhere. Don't worry.'

Windsor seemed determined to settle in for the winter at the Dowlings' house in Stanmore. Three Sundays running he locked himself in the billiard room in order to pen a long letter to his employers, explaining that he was 'indisposed but recuperating', or 'weak but convalescing', and that he expected to depart, 'God willing, in a matter of days'.

He heard nothing in return, not a word of concern or anxiety, which didn't seem to trouble him in the least. On the contrary, it confirmed the delicacy of his correspondence. The school term was almost over and Windsor had sent word to his housekeeper in Katoomba to 'dispatch some additional shirts and trousers' to save his hosts the daily obligation of washing those he had.

It had become clear by now to Mrs Dowling that her cousin's wife's brother was, as she put it, 'careless with possessions'. Each afternoon at three o'clock Windsor went out for his constitutional walk in the company of one or other of the cocker spaniels— Louisa had turned against terriers—that spent their mornings asleep on the sofa. Hearing the squeak of the front gate, she would enter his room and remove the various items—teaspoons, books from the library, the brass winding key from the grandfather clock in the hall—that in the preceding twenty-four hours had found their way into Windsor's black holdall.

One day she removed a pair of expensive goatskin gloves—
it seemed inconceivable they were Windsor's—in the belief that
Mr Dowling had bought them without telling her. Realising her
mistake, she hurried to put them back, only to be caught on the
stairs when Windsor returned early.

He noticed them in her hand. 'That is a fine pair of gloves,
Mrs Dowling,' he said. 'I shall ask your husband where he bought
them.'

It was then she understood the impulsiveness of his habit.
He stole without any recollection of what he'd stolen. Had he
been presented with the evidence he would have denied all
knowledge of it, and with some justification. Realising this, Mrs
Dowling never confronted him with the proof of his kleptomania
but simply restored the missing items to their proper places.

So Windsor went on helping himself to whatever caught his
eye, and Louisa took it back, and Isabel did her best to avoid his
daily lectures on weather and public transport. Cowed by his
constant recourse to the scriptures, neither Mrs Dowling nor her
husband could bring themselves to throw him out. (Matilda,
had she been asked, would have done it in a flash.) They
became accustomed to his presence and for a time even stopped
noticing it.

Windsor's daily routine never varied. At half past nine he
drew his curtains and assessed the day's probable meteorological
developments. Then he emerged from his bedroom, looked up
and down the landing, and locked himself in the bathroom. It
was not a long tub and Windsor, to his annoyance, could not
stretch out. He stayed there for exactly an hour and a quarter,
splashing occasionally but for the most part just wallowing in
contemplation of his kneecaps. The splashing was a useful alarm,

since he often forgot to lock the door.

He ate breakfast alone, retreated for an hour or two to the library, then intimidated Matilda into making him a sandwich. The early part of the afternoon was spent closeted in the billiard room. He followed this with a walk, after which he wandered around the house in search of someone to lecture. If Mr Dowling's shoes were being sent to the cobbler's in King Street, he made sure his went too. If Mr Dowling's shirts were collected for laundering, he added his to the pile. His undergarments, however, he kept religiously to himself, soaking them in the bathtub and leaving them to dry on his windowsill, where Isabel and her sisters could admire them while they played cricket in the garden.

He had been there a month when Isabel accidentally burst in on him bathing. She stood for a few moments transfixed. His thin hairless body was the colour of a new-born rat. There were odd folds of skin that seemed to contain no flesh at all. Though evidently startled to see her, he stood up, exposing his pallid body from top to toe. With the window behind him he looked almost transparent, like a larva in which you could see the internal organs pumping.

It occurred to Isabel to scream but she didn't. She backed out and slammed the door. There was a silence before Windsor, in a strange voice, said, 'Isabel, my dear.'

Isabel was too bewildered to answer.

'Are we alone?' he asked.

The idea of being 'alone' with Windsor in the way he seemed to be hinting was so absurd that she laughed out loud. She could as easily imagine herself alone with Mr Cyrus, the gardener, who was seventy-two.

'I think, my dear, it is your mother's day for her hair?'

Isabel caught her breath. Her mother went out for three hours every Wednesday morning to a salon in Salisbury Road to have her hair sculpted into a shape resembling a meringue.

There was something threatening in his voice. She heard his little feminine feet sucking on the bathroom tiles. 'You are a pretty girl, Isabel,' he said. 'I am fond of pretty girls.'

She turned and moved towards the stairs. The bathroom door began to open. She could hear him panting. She was already halfway down the staircase. She looked back and saw him on the landing, swaddled in a dressing gown.

'Heavens, child,' exclaimed Matilda, sweeping a pile of dust under the Persian rug in the hall. 'Whatever is the hurry?'

Windsor stared down at them. 'Would it be asking too much,' he said, gripping the banister, 'for there to be soap in the bathroom?'

~

By the time Mrs Dowling returned he was packed and gone. A short note on the mantelpiece excused his sudden departure. 'My students,' he wrote, 'can wait no longer.'

'He left very abruptly,' said Mrs Dowling. 'I hope you did nothing to offend him.'

Isabel looked up from her suitcase. 'I thought he was beyond offending.' She was angry with Windsor for his repellent suggestion and angrier with herself for not having slapped his face. The sight of that pinched rectangle of Melton overcoat scuttling down the gravel path had made her realise what a spineless creature he was. Matilda, who had no idea about the cause of the commotion, had stopped her from running after him.

'Really, dear?' said Mrs Dowling. 'I gathered his feelings were brittle.' She sat down on the edge of the bed. She had never seen half the clothes that her youngest daughter was pulling from her wardrobe. Not all of them struck her as suitable. A few were plain, even practical.

'He's a vile man,' said Isabel. 'I hope I never see him again.'

Mrs Dowling said nothing, though she was equally glad to be rid of him. Her more urgent concern, as always, was Isabel's lack of co-operation in finding a husband. She was now eighteen years old, an age at which each of her sisters had already made a choice, or at least assented to the choice made by her mother. None of those marriages, so far as Mrs Dowling could see, had turned out badly. Numerous children had been produced and others were imminent. Isabel alone had resisted all her best efforts to identify a suitable mate. And now she was abandoning them again to visit her uncle in Emu Plains. This time she was going without Matilda.

'You know, Isabel,' she said, 'I really think it would be better if you wrote ahead. The house may be empty.'

'Uncle John is always home. And even if he's not, the front door is never locked.'

Her mother put a hand to her mouth. 'Isabel! You wouldn't break into an empty house?'

'It wouldn't be breaking in. And I know he wouldn't mind.'

'Then you know more about my brother than I do.'

'I should do, Mama. You never visit him.'

It seemed to her mother that Isabel was packing a large amount of clothes for such a short stay. 'But he visits us, dear.

Why should we impose ourselves on him? Besides, you know your father doesn't travel well.'

Isabel did know this. She also knew it was a temperamental rather than a physical aversion. Her father became distressed at the prospect of journeying further than ten miles in any direction. This confined him to a circle that stretched from the low-water mark at Coogee beach to the outskirts of Parramatta.

Mrs Dowling went on, 'I'm sure your father would not approve if he thought—'

'Then please don't tell him.' Isabel bent down and hugged her mother. 'Believe me, Mama, Uncle John likes to be surprised. He'd be offended if I suddenly wrote to him before setting out.'

'If you're sure, Isabel. Only—'

'Of course I'm sure.'

Mrs Dowling loved but did not pretend to understand her youngest daughter. She didn't know how a string of presentable suitors, any one of whom would in her opinion have made a perfectly satisfactory son-in-law, could all be found wanting. She had watched dozens of young hopefuls arrive, deliver their flowers, drink their tea and depart, never to be seen again. She worried that Isabel had set her sights too high. 'I had intended,' she said wistfully, 'to have a little party.'

Isabel pretended not to hear. 'May I take some roses?' she asked.

'Will they survive the trip?'

'They have before.'

'In that case, take as many as you like. John was always fond of roses.' She smiled. 'You're right, dear. I really should visit him one day, if only I could persuade your father to accompany me.'

'Nonsense, Mama. Go alone. Matilda will make sure Papa doesn't starve.'

Louisa Dowling laughed. She couldn't fathom Isabel but sometimes she almost admired her.

'I'm sorry I'll miss the party,' said Isabel. She wasn't sorry at all. She started towards the door. She had arrangements to make, shoes to find, coaches to book. 'I'll give Uncle John your love.'

⁓

Miles was as nimble and reckless as he had been at seven. He hung upside down to adjust the lights and shake out the backdrops. He scrambled up ropes one-handed and never wore a safety harness. The skies he painted were so realistic that the clouds seemed to float by.

Tobias Smith's notebook was driving him mad. He could understand the words but not the thinking behind them. There seemed to be a hidden meaning to every sentence. Miles combed the shelves of the public library, reading everything he could about flying. He scoured bookshops and flea markets and pored over catalogues of deceased estates. He sat in the reading room of the Mechanics' Institute copying drawings of George Barclay's 1849 monoplane glider, in which a melon-shaped aerial car was suspended from a large bat's wing, and Henri Canteloupe's 1853 bird-plane, a rigid fuselage sandwiched between two swept-back falcon-shaped wings. Every evening he returned to Smith's notebook.

Then one wet day in July he came across an engraving of Louis Pernod's *Planophore*, which in August 1871 flew 131 feet before the Société de Navigation Aérienne in the Tuileries in Paris.

Pernod's model was twelve inches long, with a rigid fuselage, diamond-shaped wings and tailplane. It was driven by a rear-mounted eight-inch propeller powered by a rubber band and bore a striking resemblance to one of Tobias Smith's own sketches.

Miles could scarcely believe something so momentous had happened just three years earlier. Here was the spur he'd been waiting for. He decided to build it.

In the theatre workshop he had all the tools and timber he required and as much cloth as he could want. It took him two months. The rough skills he used for tables and battlements were not the ones he needed to build a flying machine. But slowly the plane began to take shape. Miles's version of the *Planophore* was made of raw silk stretched over timber rods and measured nine inches from nose to tail. On 3 September 1874 it flew twenty-eight feet with a light following wind across a grass paddock in Dulwich Hill. Miles was thrilled. He skipped home through the dust and dirt of Canterbury Road.

He followed it with another half as long again, built of the same materials. But in extending the fuselage Miles had altered the centre of gravity. On 23 November the plane flew a mere twelve feet before crashing. It was hardly a flight at all; he stamped on it in disgust.

Miles's worktable was strewn with diagrams he had copied in the reading room of the Mechanics' Institute: wing sections, plans and elevations of the fuselage, intricate details of the propeller mechanism. But they felt remote, sterile, like actors' marks on an empty stage.

He began to build another *Planophore* incorporating some of the ideas he'd found in Tobias Smith's notebook. It was more ambitious than Pernod's original. This one was three feet long and substituted linen for silk. Instead of rubber bands Miles used ligatures made of kangaroo tendon. He gave it rectangular rather than diamond-shaped wings and added a shark's fin to the tailplane. He arrived at the theatre each morning at seven or half past, firing up the old cast-iron boiler and sharpening his tools before starting work on his machine. Often he stayed until midnight; sometimes he slept there, waking at dawn to find the caretaker squinting at him through his wire-rimmed spectacles. He worked feverishly, sifting through piles of timber before choosing a piece that suited his purpose. Mrs Gwilym hardly saw him for days on end. They ate together only at weekends. The rest of the time he'd come home to find a plate of cold cuts left for him under an upturned pudding basin.

In the beginning Mrs Gwilym would ask him how it was going, make encouraging remarks, refer to men she had known with passions for old pots and seashells. But Miles's passion seemed all-consuming. His intensity unnerved her. He was convinced that this, the Australian *Planophore*, was the machine Tobias Smith was dreaming of. Now it had fallen to him to build it.

It was early autumn before the plane was finished. Miles walked all over Sydney in search of a suitable launching place and finally settled on a low hill behind the beach at Maroubra. The breeze was much stronger than he'd imagined. A sudden shower drenched the linen, which shrank as it dried. There was too little tension in the tendons that powered the propeller. But Miles did not have the patience to wait. The machine veered out of his hand and fell like a stone, disintegrating on impact.

He wandered home in a daze. He would have burned the notebook if Mrs Gwilym hadn't snatched it from the fire. When

Briggs suggested that one of his clouds was too dark, Miles threw down his paintbrush, removed his apron and announced he was quitting.

Some days after Isabel had left for her uncle's house in Emu Plains, Mrs Dowling discovered a letter. It had been propped against the brass balloonist and his dog but the wind had blown it down. 'Dearest Mama,' it began,

> I told you I was going to visit Uncle John. What I forgot to mention was that I am not going there directly. I've decided to see the country. I don't mean the river at Parramatta but something further afield. I thought I might go to Melbourne but now I'm not sure. I would very much like to see Adelaide too, and the Murray River.
>
> Of course I expect you to be horrified, and for Papa to announce that he will mount an expedition to fetch me back. But I have no wish to be fetched and so I won't tell you where I'm going, although I shall certainly write at every opportunity. You mustn't worry as I have plenty of money and an atlas, so there is no likelihood of my getting lost. You also mustn't think I'm mad, or running off with a stableboy, or was lured away by anything other than curiosity and restlessness, which is all quite satisfactory in a boy, who can buy a horse and go out exploring, but very frustrating in a girl, who is expected to lie down on the settee until she feels better.
>
> Mama, you will probably suspect a conspiracy and blame Uncle John, but he did nothing more than lend me

twenty pounds when I asked for it (I didn't tell him what it was for) and will be as surprised as you to hear the news. I could write another page and say some obnoxious things about Windsor but I'm sure you wouldn't believe them, so I shall stop here and say I love you and will come home when I'm ready and I promise not to get married without telling you.

Isabel xx

'It's my brother's fault,' cried Louisa.

'Don't worry,' her husband reassured her. 'We'll mount an expedition. She can't have gone far. We'll have her back in a day or two.'

Isabel's sisters were indignant and were all for setting the black trackers onto her. But her parents, after fuming for a day, accepted the news with surprising equanimity. They realised they were powerless. And of all their daughters—in fact of all the people they had ever met below the age of thirty—they knew that Isabel offered the least encouragement for thinking she wouldn't do what she had set out to do. They closed her bedroom door and awaited her return.

Isabel's travels took her clockwise in a great arc from the Snowy Mountains to the Warrumbungles. She had hardly been gone a week when a child stole her mirror brush. When she caught glimpses of herself in bathrooms and shop windows, she couldn't help noticing how she was changing. The sun turned her arms as dark as the timber that stood ringbarked on the Murrumbidgee flats. Freckles covered her face. She wondered if her parents would recognise her.

The soil became redder, the towns scruffier, the wind drier. The horizon appeared to bow like the curve of the ocean. Often she found herself staring up at the sky and remembering how Windsor had pontificated about flying machines. The thought of him still made her angry; the smugness of his opinion on any subject was enough to make her argue the opposite. Flying seemed such an incongruous dream in a land of sheep and dirt. And yet, she thought, was there anywhere on earth with more sky, and less to show for it? Wasn't this the *obvious* place in which to fly?

There were accidents, misadventures, a snakebite in Grenfell, a plague of horseflies in Yass, fevers and food poisoning, dust storms and bridges washed away; blacks reduced to beggars in fringe camps; more than Isabel had bargained for when she left her parents' red-brick house in Railway Avenue.

It was taken for granted that a young woman travelling alone was in desperate need of a companion. She was forever answering questions, inventing alibis. The questioners became more irksome; she was visiting her uncle, she said, then her fiance, then her husband. In Young a prospector boasted of the gold dust in the stitching of his boots; he followed Isabel to her hotel and took the room next door. She didn't sleep all night and escaped down the back stairs before it was light.

She kept only the most circumspect souvenirs: fragments of coloured rock, a pair of gumnuts, the lustrous red tail-feather of a black cockatoo, things she could carry easily in the bottom of her suitcase. Sometimes one piece had to go to make room for another. Her memory followed suit: vivid recollections of one place, others almost forgotten. The country was too big to picture it all. But what she remembered most was the sky.

From the plains she travelled south through Coolah, Gulgong, Lithgow. She woke up one morning and recognised the eucalyptus haze of the Blue Mountains. She was in a town that lost its future when the toll road moved north. All that remained was a hotel, a courthouse and a crooked row of terraces. Isabel had landed there by accident. The hotel was crumbling around her. She had heard mice in the ceiling. No-one had dusted in ten years.

Isabel had always been a restless sleeper; all night she moved around the bed as if searching for something. The hem of her nightdress was around her waist; her thick hair tangled and knotted like a bird's nest. She threw back the top sheet. The window was wide open; there had once been iron bars but they had been removed.

For an instant she thought that someone had been in the room with her. Her scuffed and battered suitcase was lying open, some of her belongings were lying on the floor at the foot of the bed. But the key was still in the door.

Next morning was Saturday. A hot wind was bowling dust along the main street. There were a dozen or so men beneath her window jabbering about the races. Isabel dressed and hurried downstairs. 'Which races?' she asked.

'Emu Plains,' said a man with a red moustache. A cart rolled to a halt outside the hotel.

'Have you room for me?' asked Isabel.

The man looked her over. 'We'll make room for you, girlie,' he said.

Horatio's Boomerang Brandy, obtainable in bottles, flasks and half-flasks, hastened recovery from influenza. It said so on the label, in newspaper advertisements and in black letters three feet high on a hundred walls across Sydney. Miles had read them all; now that he'd given up flying he had nothing better to do.

Professors of anatomy vouched for it, as did many of their counterparts in law and the classics, not to mention thirsty businessmen, their wives, servants and gardeners, the manufacturer himself and the twenty-odd employees he paid to distil and bottle the elixir in a dank, windowless factory abutting the railway line at Newtown.

A number of respected politicians who didn't have influenza found a half-flask of Horatio's Boomerang Brandy an invaluable tonic during long parliamentary sittings. The editor of the *Sydney Morning Herald* and most of his staff spoke admiringly of the stuff. It was big with barrowmen, street hawkers, stonesmiths, blacksmiths and locksmiths.

The governor was rumoured to have several bottles laid up in a trunk. There were casks of it in the cellars at Victoria Barracks. The chief justice was not a drinker but his wife was and she drank nothing else. If water ever ran short in a drought, Sydney would probably get by on Horatio's Boomerang Brandy.

Miles was swigging from a half-flask when a cart drawn by two grey geldings trundled past displaying a slogan on a canvas roller:

HORATIO'S BOOMERANG BRANDY has been
Unstintingly Recommended by the Medical Faculty
as a NOURISHING STIMULANT to Counteract

the Effects of INFLUENZA DROPSY GOUT TIREDNESS
DESPONDENCY and other MALEVOLENT CONDITIONS
of the BODY and SPIRIT

It was the first of April, a month since he'd quit his job and
a year to the day since the *Central Plains Herald* had celebrated the
fateful rebirth of Tobias Smith. Flecks of white cloud drifted
across a clear blue sky. Miles was climbing the hill from
Woolloomooloo. He'd been down to the wharves and had just
watched six pelicans fighting over some fish guts. When they'd
finished eating, the birds tumbled off the wharf and flapped away
across the harbour. Now they were over the city, their black and
white wings outstretched, rising on the slowly turning screw of a
thermal. Miles marvelled at the contrast: down here they were fat
stupid things, gobbling and fighting over piles of stinking offal;
up there they were graceful, silent creatures, gliding along an
invisible thread.

He grimaced as he swallowed. Horatio's was the worst
brandy money could buy but it was keenly priced and Miles
wasn't a discriminating drinker. He understood Smith's dejection.
He stuffed the flask in his pocket as the cart drove by.

The two grey geldings were treating the gentle gradient like
the foothills of a mountain, snorting and hanging their heads and
dragging their hairy heels. The driver, a dapper little man in a
black felt hat, took no notice. He sat hunched over the reins,
apparently fast asleep.

As the horses continued to climb, he shook himself awake
and gave the roller several rough churns. The first advertisement
disappeared and another swung into place:

MIND YOUR IN'ARDS

WHY?

Because there is no Line of Business in which the Public
may be more Imposed upon by Unscrupulous Persons
than the LIQUOR TRADE

WATCH YOUR HEALTH

Drink only HORATIO'S BOOMERANG BRANDY

As the hill became steeper, the horses slowed until the cart
was hardly moving. The driver shouted some half-hearted abuse,
which had no effect, and then hung his head over the side of the
cart. 'Give us a shove will you, son?'

Miles wasn't listening.

'Son, give us a bloody shove, eh?'

Miles soon caught up. 'What about the horses?'

'Buggered, mate. Look at 'em. Just to the top of the hill.
She'll be fine from there.'

'You must be joking.'

'Does it look like I'm joking? Jesus, I'd push it myself only…'
He cut himself short. 'Go on, lad. Bloody whacked, these two.
Been at it all day.'

Miles didn't know a lot about horses but it didn't take a
jockey to know that these two were putting it on. He reached for
the harness.

'What are you doing? Get your bloody hands off 'em!'

The horses broke into a reluctant trot.

'Whoa there!' shouted the driver, leaping out of his seat. For
a man who'd only just woken up he was quick on his feet.

Miles was trotting alongside. It looked for a moment as
though the driver was going to jump off. 'Left around the corner,

son,' he shouted. 'Don't give 'em a sight of the water or I'll never get the buggers back.'

The risk of that seemed negligible. They turned the corner, the road levelled out and after a while the horses resumed their weary trudge towards Darlinghurst.

'You might as well hop on,' said the driver.

Miles grabbed a corner of the cart and swung himself up. Sitting next to him, he could see that the man was less stylish than he appeared. The suit he was wearing turned out, on closer inspection, to be a combination of three different outfits: a pair of dark pin-striped trousers, a double-breasted herringbone coat and an undertaker's black waistcoat, all fused under a layer of Sydney grime. 'O'Hare,' he said, laying his hand out horizontally, as if he expected a pound note to be dropped into it.

'McGinty,' said Miles.

O'Hare pondered for a minute or two. 'Not, by any chance, related to the actress…whatsername?'

'Eliza.'

'That's 'er.'

'No,' said Miles. He wasn't in a mood to talk.

O'Hare shrugged. 'Bloody good they say she was.'

They reached William Street and O'Hare turned right towards the city. He saw Miles looking at the canvas roller and gestured over his shoulder. 'Go on, son,' he said, 'give it a whirl. Bloody thing doesn't move by itself.'

Miles reached behind him and rotated the crank half a dozen times until a new slogan came up:

HORATIO'S BOOMERANG BRANDY
is Made from the Finest Ingredients

Praised by MEDICAL AUTHORITIES

NO IMPURITIES

Do not Soil your Lips with Inferior Brands

'Did you come up with them yourself?' asked Miles.

'Me? No, lad. Straight from head office, this lot. Adver-tize-ments is what they're called. Make a man do with his wits asleep what he wouldn't dream of doing with 'em awake, that's the idea of 'em.'

Miles watched two men emerge from an alley. They stopped talking and stared, their gaze fixed on the moving slogan.

O'Hare uttered a sardonic grunt. It didn't matter to him whether people took any notice or not. His work was assessed in miles, and the number he travelled was determined not by him but by the horses. This arrangement satisfied O'Hare, who would happily have continued driving his advertising cart in ever-diminishing circles until, some months or years down the track, the horses refused to venture beyond the perimeter of Hyde Park.

But Sydney was drinking all it could. The future of Horatio's Boomerang Brandy lay with the parched populations to the west. A great, untapped market beckoned and O'Hare had been ordered to go looking for it. He had in his pocket a map indicat-ing the settled areas from Parramatta to the Nepean River. He was obliged to set off in two days' time. He didn't fancy the thought of travelling alone.

The sandstone walls of the grammar school burned red in the afternoon sun.

'You know, son,' said O'Hare. 'You're a handy-looking feller. I could use a bit of help.'

'Doing what?' asked Miles. As far as he could see there was

nothing to O'Hare's job but waking up from time to time and turning the wooden crank.

'This and that,' said O'Hare. 'We're heading out west in a day or two: Richmond, Parramatta, Emu Plains if we're lucky. Wouldn't mind a bit of company.' He gave the smaller of the two horses a flick with his whip. 'Any good with horses?'

'Emu Plains?' he asked. It might as well have been Goondiwindi or Timbuktu.

'That's where I'm heading.'

'I'll come,' said Miles.

'You won't mind passing me the flask?'

Miles pulled the flat green bottle out of his pocket and handed it to O'Hare, who held it up to the light before letting it drop. 'Horse piss,' he said. 'I wouldn't wash me boots in it.'

For a day or two Mrs Gwilym put Miles to work. She had him wash down the paintwork and sluice the yard. In the evening she fattened him up on bacon and pickled onions. He had saved a few pounds, and spent eighteen shillings and six on a pair of Geelong tweed trousers and thirty-five shillings on a beaver overcoat. He sewed five pounds in a pocket and hid the rest in a drawer for Mrs Gwilym to find when he'd gone.

'Don't forget this,' she shouted, throwing Tobias Smith's notebook after him as he turned the corner into Stanley Street. Miles hesitated for a moment before picking it up.

The racetrack at Emu Plains was a scandalous place. Scandalous races were won at scandalous odds. A few months earlier, Bold as Brass, twelve lengths ahead coming out of the final bend, pulled up seventy yards from home and walked in last. The year before, A King for a Day, the Tamworth flier, went lame at the sound of the starter's gun and once a donkey from Muswellbrook trotted home at 150 to 1 with a one-armed butcher's boy in the saddle.

Punters came over the mountains from Oberon, Lithgow, Portland, Wallerawang, galloping down dusty red roads or hanging off the backs of bullock carts with their coats in their laps. The bookies, sharp-eyed, dark-skinned men in neckerchiefs and woollen waistcoats, stood and watched like eagles over a stubble field.

It was almost a quarter to three when Isabel reached Emu Plains. A broken wheel had cost them two hours. While it was being mended, the men passed around a bottle of rum. She was glad to see the large oleander bush bursting through the railings of her uncle's garden.

The house was empty. There was no smoke from the chimneys; the windows were shut. The doctor's buggy was in the shed and his horse was in the stables. Isabel guessed he'd be at the racecourse. She left her suitcase on the porch and headed for the track.

By the time she got there, most of the races had already been run. The last card had been called. Isabel hurried past the seated enclosure, where several men in black suits had canes across their knees, as though ready to leap up and strike the flanks of passing horses. It would have surprised her to see the doctor there but she looked around anyway. She recognised his colleagues, Sproule and L'Estrange, sitting side by side under identical silk hats but there was no sign of her uncle, who liked to stand on the rails, where he could feel the ground shake and look his horse in the eye.

Then she spotted him. Dr Galbraith was short, squat and ruddy-faced and liked to wear blue serge suits, double-breasted with mother-of-pearl buttons. Today he was dressed in a silver-grey jacket and herringbone trousers, set off with a bottle-green billycock hat.

Isabel shouted but her uncle didn't hear. She had to elbow her way through the mass of punters pressing notes and coins into the damp palms of bookies who were loudly calling their odds for the last race through a fog of tobacco smoke. She was almost upon him when he turned round. 'Isabel,' he exclaimed, 'I was beginning to wonder if you'd ever arrive.'

She threw her arms around his neck, shrugging off the stares that greeted any female interloper. She had expected him to be more surprised. She'd written, without giving him much idea of when she was coming. Much as he loved his niece, Dr Galbraith seemed mildly perturbed that, after months away, she hadn't waited a few more minutes. 'Wouldn't you be more comfort-able—'

'No I wouldn't,' she cried. There was almost no time to get to the bookies. 'What's your money on?'

'Isabel, you're not going to—'

'Just a pound,' she said.

'A pound!'

'Come on, uncle'—she grabbed his wrist—'or it'll be too late.'

'Velocipede,' he began. He would have continued, 'is the outsider—anyone but her.' But Isabel was already off, pushing through the crowd, which closed behind her.

The punters had vanished from the bookies' enclosure. A couple were still calling out odds while the others rummaged in their satchels. Isabel rushed up to a man in a mustard jacket and slapped her pound note into his hand.

A small dachshund that had been smuggled past the stewards was scampering back and forth between the rails. Its owner went after it. A steward rushed from the crowd and chased them both with a switch. Fifty yards away the horses were being shouldered to the tape. Galbraith looked around for his niece. A surge from the crowd pinned him to the rail. He heard the crack of the starter's gun.

Pharaoh's Daughter hit the first bend a length in front, followed by Tar Barrel, Jack of Hearts and Iron Duke, with Velocipede, a 40 to 1 shot from Dubbo, already a distant last owing to some confusion in the stalls. By the end of the straight Iron Duke was sitting on the leader's shoulder, with Tar Barrel and Jack of Hearts losing interest and Velocipede, carrying Isabel's pound note and not much else, falling away with every stride.

Isabel was so far back she could hardly see. She glanced over her shoulder. The bookies' area was deserted. She saw a soapbox and jumped on it.

There were now a dozen lengths between Velocipede and the next horse and half a dozen more before the bunch snorting and barging for the front. The doctor screwed up his stub and was backing out when a hot gust of wind blew out of nowhere, bending the yellow box trees that clustered at one end of the track. The branches trembled and the trunks shook and a cloud of red dust barrelled down the home straight, blinding the jockeys and causing the horses to scatter and pull up in fright until only one was left. Velocipede was lumbering round the bend so far behind the field that by the time she was into the straight the dust storm had blown itself out and the track was clear and there wasn't another horse between her and the winning post.

'Isabel,' Galbraith called out as the crowd fell away. She was pushing towards him, clutching the dirty bundle of banknotes in her fist. Forty pounds was more than she had ever laid eyes on before. It was hot and greasy in her fingers: a roll of crumpled banknotes that had been through a thousand hands before hers, bought bricks and horses and kidney pills, settled debts and been gambled away at cards.

'You didn't?' said Galbraith.

'I did!'

They joined the tide moving towards the gates. Galbraith persuaded Isabel to let him hold on to the money until they were home, though the pickpockets took more interest in him than in her.

'Aren't you going to ask me where I've been?' she said. 'Aren't you fascinated?'

'Of course I'm fascinated.'

'You don't sound it.'

'I was waiting for you to decide to tell me.'

'Is Mama well? I've written often.'

Galbraith held onto his billycock hat, which was in danger of being knocked off. 'The last your mother told me she was well.'

'No need to ask about Papa,' said Isabel. 'He's always well. And my sisters?'

'Everyone's in the best of health. Even the dogs, I'm told, have never been better. They've been very impatient for your return.' He smiled. 'The dogs, especially.'

It was nearly five o'clock. Dark clouds were piling on top of the mountains. There was rain on the way.

'Do I look different?' she asked.

Galbraith looked sideways at his niece. She was taller and thinner. He hadn't noticed her before to have freckles. The backs of her hands were brown. Her fair hair tumbled from under a frazzled straw hat. She wore a long lilac dress with a grey button-down jacket; both had been washed more often than was good for them. Galbraith had never seen his niece looking anything less than elegant but there was a slight scruffiness to her now that he found endearing. 'A little wiser,' he said.

'Now that I'm back,' she said, 'I want to do something surprising.'

'Then perhaps,' he teased, 'you should marry one of the young men who are so devoted to you.'

'They are devoted to my mother. They're merely fond of me.'

They stopped to allow Dr Galbraith to admire the climbing roses that his gardener had succeeded in coaxing over a metal arch standing in the front garden. It occurred to him to ask his gardener to erect another arch. The pair would then be symmetrical. One on its own looked arbitrary.

'Your roses have black spot,' said Isabel. 'You should sack your gardener.'

'He's too old to sack. I would feel obliged to pay him a pension.'

Isabel frowned. Her uncle's little joke about marriage had reminded her of what she could expect when she got home. 'Have you ever been in love?' she asked.

'You've asked me that before.'

'You never give a straight answer.'

'The straight answer is yes. Does that satisfy you?'

'I don't want a straight answer. Is my forty pounds still there?'

Galbraith felt in his jacket pocket. 'Yes.'

The money, though she was glad to have it, now seemed less exciting than when they had started out. She wished she had taken it in sovereigns.

'Why, Isabel,' said her uncle. 'Have *you* ever been in love?'

'Never for longer than a week.'

It was quite cold but Galbraith showed no hurry to go indoors. He wandered slowly among the roses, though by now it was almost dark. 'I was in love, a very long time ago, with a girl called Ada. She was younger than me, rather plain, some might say—'

'But not to you?'

'No. To me she was unspeakably lovely. It was in Sofala. I had gone to work on the goldfields. I had something of a knack for bone-setting. Such skills were much in demand.'

'And Ada?'

'A chemist's daughter, as I thought. He owned a dispensary. Ada had blue eyes and the longest hair I have ever seen. She used to sit on it. One day she helped me with a surgical operation. I removed a tumour from a young man. Sadly it was far advanced and he died shortly afterwards. That day Ada and I had lunch together. Herrings, I think, of which there was always an abundant supply on the goldfields. She was an avid reader and back then I knew some verses by heart. She insisted on being my assistant when I couldn't operate alone.'

'Did you kiss?'

'Often. Too often, I'm afraid. She had a very silky manner.

A gold crucifix hung maddeningly around her neck. I thought she shared my feelings. I was convinced we were in love. Fortunately I didn't act upon it.'

'She jilted you?'

'It might have been better if she had. I was on the point of asking the chemist, in whose company I had spent many enjoyable evenings, whether he consented to my proposing to his daughter. Thank God I didn't.'

'She was his wife,' said Isabel. It was now so dark that she could not see his face. But she saw him take a handkerchief from his pocket. He made a meal, she thought, of blowing his nose.

⁓

Dr Galbraith owned one of the stranger houses in Emu Plains. Besides the pink walls and crenellations and the dovecot protruding from the middle of the roof, it had a series of oval windows sunk, like eyeballs, into the walls. A gabled porch jutted out, supported by two sandstone pillars as big as tram wheels. It was here that Isabel had left her suitcase.

A coach lamp was attached to one of the pillars by an iron collar which bled streaks of rust. The state of the lamp suggested it was no longer in use. Nocturnal visitors had to make do with the light from the hall that penetrated the stained-glass window above the door. On the other pillar was a handle connected to a smooth leather strap which disappeared into the column and re-emerged just below the roof, where a series of rusty cogs, rotating on perpendicular axes, culminated in a hammer and bell that collided with a dull thud. There were several other devices in various states of disrepair. The only one that worked was a brass knocker in the shape of a lion's head. The door, in any case, was never locked, rendering the whole lot superfluous.

'Supper will be simple, I'm afraid,' said Galbraith, holding the door open for Isabel. 'I didn't anticipate your coming.'

'Don't worry,' she said. 'I'm not hungry.'

Isabel always found herself holding her breath entering her uncle's house after an absence. He was a cultured professional gentleman of late middle age living alone. His house reflected all the eccentricity that such a description implied. It was dark, untidy, lacked fresh air and decent curtains; was overstuffed with furniture and had been expensively (but not recently) painted in the wrong colours. His taste was by and large as rash as his sister's was refined. Dr Galbraith didn't much care what sort of a house he lived in as long as he had a garden to look out on, and as long as there was plenty of room for his acquisitions.

Galbraith was a fine doctor. His delicate skills and affable manner were much sought after by patients frightened or repelled by the cooler expertise of Sproule and L'Estrange. He wryly diagnosed in himself a mania for mechanical objects, and these now filled every corner of the house: machines for sewing, for polishing, for crushing garlic and punching holes in leather belts, electrical alarms, pianolas, even a clockwork device for turning the pages of a book.

Isabel was always impatient to see them. She loved trying to guess what they were for. She kicked off her shoes and walked straight into her uncle's study. 'What's this?' she called out. She was staring at a large timber crate painted on all four sides with the words: 'GALBRAITH. EMU PLAINS.'

'That,' said Galbraith, 'is a bicycle, or will be when I can find someone to put it together.'

'And what is a bicycle?'

'I am assured it will make walking obsolete.'

Isabel peered at it through the holes in the crate. It smelt of grease and metal. 'It can't be that hard,' she said. 'Are you sure we can't do it ourselves?'

'Are you handy with a spanner?'

'Of course,' she said, though she'd never held one in her life.

'In that case we should have no difficulty.'

'Tomorrow's Sunday,' said Isabel. 'We'll do it then.'

O'Hare's grey geldings managed to idle away the best part of a month from the Glebe toll pike to the old soldiers' barracks at Emu Plains.

Time was immaterial to O'Hare, to whom each day was like every other day. He hardly bothered to shave. His whiskers grew unevenly, the left cheek markedly shaggier than the right, his upper lip almost bare and his chin bristling like a wheat sheaf. He was used to the horses; he didn't care how long they took to get where they were going, how many shoes they kicked or how many bags of oats they emptied. The makers of Horatio's Boomerang Brandy paid him four shillings a day, plus expenses. That made them accomplices.

O'Hare obeyed his instructions to the letter, turning his canvas roller (or instructing Miles to turn it) every half-hour while it was daylight, regardless of whether there was anyone to see it. They stayed at cheap inns along the way and never went hungry.

The older man wasn't much of a talker. He spent whole mornings smoking his pipe in silence. He gave the impression that life had given him a great deal to think about. They grew close in a distant sort of way.

Sometimes Miles walked behind, wanting the sky to himself. He'd stop and stare at flocks of galahs, at hawks quivering over bone-dry paddocks. By the time he looked for O'Hare the cart would be half a mile away, a smudge of dirt rolling towards the horizon. O'Hare was a bit of a bird-watcher himself. He didn't pretend to be an expert. He'd once seen an albatross over the dunes at Portsea and never forgotten it.

On days when O'Hare didn't fancy moving on, Miles would find himself reaching instinctively for Tobias Smith's notebook. His thoughts kept coming back to the pelicans; how they were transformed in flight from the waddling, flat-footed things he'd seen on the wharf. He began to sense some plain and simple truth lay hidden in Smith's mad scrawl, an underlying principle he'd find if he searched hard enough. He knew he'd come too far to give up now.

'All this bloody reading,' O'Hare said one day. 'Where's it going?'

It was a sunny day and they were picnicking on the banks of the Nepean River. O'Hare had laid his hands on some bacon, which they would shortly be eating between slabs of Miles's damper.

'I mean,' he went on, 'is it fame you're after, or money, or what is it?'

Miles was sitting between the roots of a huge river gum. 'There's a secret to it,' he said. 'I want to find it.'

'And you reckon it's in that book of yours?'

'Could be.'

'I'll tell you the secret, son.' O'Hare turned his back on Miles and slapped his bony arse. 'Feathers. That's the secret. We haven't got 'em.'

'And what do you know about it?' said Miles.

'I've been around, lad,' O'Hare answered mysteriously. 'I've seen things.'

Miles stood up and heaped more embers on the fire. There were pieces of mottled river-gum bark among the ashes and the disturbance caused a few blackened shreds to spiral up into the branches.

Neither of them spoke for several minutes. Miles fussed with the fire while O'Hare wandered down to the river and splashed some water on his face. When he returned he looked different. He had wiped his face on his sleeve but a few drops still glistened on his forehead. He had the expression of someone who'd just reached a difficult decision.

'Ever heard of a bloke called Sheridan?' he asked.

'Wrote plays,' said Miles.

O'Hare looked surprised. 'Never knew that. Thomas Sheridan of Geelong. Ten thousand acres. Ran sheep. Mates with the governor. The pair of 'em went shooting together.'

'Different Sheridan,' said Miles.

'Well, lad, this one'—he hesitated, as if having second thoughts about what he was going to say—'this one fancied he could fly.'

Miles imagined he knew about every would-be flier who had tried his luck in the colonies. There weren't many: a deranged clergyman in New Zealand who jumped off a cliff holding an albatross's wings; an engineer in the Indian army who was killed when his balloon was shot down by frightened sepoys. 'What happened?' he asked.

O'Hare lit a cigarette and watched the match burn out. It was clear he wasn't going to be rushed.

'Did you see him fly?' asked Miles.

'Not exactly,' said O'Hare.

'Well?'

O'Hare put the cigarette in his mouth and inhaled so deeply that his bloodshot eyeballs appeared to cloud over. He drew the smoke down to the bottom of his lungs for what seemed an eternity before letting it out. 'Mr Thomas bloody Sheridan built himself a box kite. A big bastard. Made of canvas and birch. Wind blew up before he was ready. Got his foot caught in the rope. Dragged him halfway across the estate. Skinned him raw. Two broken ribs. Dropped him in a lake.' A look of regret passed across his haggard face. 'Bugger would have drowned,' he said, 'if I hadn't fished him out.' O'Hare removed his cigarette and rubbed it between his fingers until the unsmoked tobacco burst from the paper.

'A kite?' said Miles.

O'Hare nodded. 'A kite is what Sheridan called it. As big as a hansom cab, with more strings than a square rigger.'

'And you saw it fly?'

'No, son. I saw it crash.'

'But it must have flown…'

O'Hare tossed away the crushed remains of his cigarette. 'If you say so.'

Miles walked slowly around the river gum. It was an ancient tree with a gnarled red trunk covered with knots and tumours. Two lorikeets were chattering in the upper branches. They swooped out of the tree and flew off in a blur of brilliant green and red.

'It's logical,' said Miles. 'It must have been up for you to see it come down.'

'Don't know anything about logical,' O'Hare answered gruffly. 'All I'm telling you, lad, is what I saw.'

If Miles had heard the story from anyone but O'Hare—from Wolunsky, for instance—he wouldn't have believed it.

'Are you certain?'

'You mean, was I drunk? No, son. But I was soaking bloody wet when I'd finished.'

There was more to Sheridan's story than O'Hare knew. It reminded Miles of a sketch in Tobias Smith's notebook of a string of different-sized box kites attached to one another. Smith was convinced that, if the kites were sturdy enough, such an assembly would be capable of lifting the weight of a man. Miles had never taken the idea seriously. He'd thought of kites as toys and was captivated by the bird-planes of Barclay and Canteloupe, and by Pernod's *Planophore*, not to mention Smith's own propeller plane. He'd thrown all his energy into building one and had nothing to show for it. Whereas Sheridan had hitched his efforts to the kite and had succeeded in getting himself airborne.

Suddenly it was obvious to Miles that Pernod and Barclay and Canteloupe were barking up the wrong tree, trying to attach a propeller to a machine that couldn't fly. Sheridan had proved that a box kite could carry a man. If Miles could build a better box kite, with some kind of rudder to steer it, he'd have the basis of a flying machine.

O'Hare was crouching beside the fire. 'You see what I'm saying, son? It's a game for idiots. It's standing in a paddock and

baring your arse to a bull.' He began to rake the ashes from the
buried damper. 'Now where's that bloody bacon?'

Isabel and her uncle spent the next morning trying to make sense
of the bars and brackets and nuts and bolts that fell out of the
crate when they opened it. Galbraith had come across the
machine—a 'Genuine English Safety Bicycle' manufactured by
Holsworthy & Sons of Taunton, Somerset—advertised for twenty
pounds in the pages of the *Australian Home Companion and Illustrated
Weekly Magazine*. The importer had not thought to include a set
of instructions.

After lunch they tried again. But nothing they made bore any
resemblance to the picture of the Holsworthy bicycle Galbraith
had seen in the magazine.

'Fancy that,' said the doctor, beckoning Isabel to the window
of his study. A cart was trundling slowly past the front gate, with
a hand-painted slogan on a canvas screen.

It is an AUTHENTIC FACT
That Thousands of VALUABLE SOULS have been Sacrificed
to the Consumption of PERNICIOUS LIQUOR
Drink to your HEALTH
With HORATIO'S BOOMERANG BRANDY
You will not Regret it
LEADING CLERGYMEN COMMEND IT

'An apt message for the Sabbath,' said Galbraith. 'I wonder if our
own Mr Ransom is among its supporters.'

At first the cart seemed to be driving itself, but as it emerged from behind the doctor's oleander bush Isabel saw that there were two people on board, a little old man slouched over the reins and his strapping companion standing behind the translucent screen. The slogan was crooked and the second man was attempting to straighten it. With the afternoon sun behind him he was like a shadow puppet floating by.

Isabel had noticed two empty decanters in her uncle's study. 'I hope you haven't been sacrificing your soul to pernicious liquor,' she said.

'Only my riches,' said Galbraith. 'Now, where were we?'

On Monday after breakfast Isabel walked into town to enlist the help of William Jolly the blacksmith. Jolly couldn't promise to arrive before evening. At twenty-two minutes past seven, just as Isabel and her uncle were sitting down to dinner, there was a terrifying bang on the front door.

'Mr Jolly,' said Galbraith, 'we're just having dinner. I don't suppose you'd—'

'Join you?' asked the blacksmith. 'I don't mind if I do.'

Jolly was a barrel-shaped torso suspended from two enormous shoulders. Coils of black hair burst from his collar and sleeves. His legs were comically short but it was likely no-one had ever pointed this out. He wore a sour look that said blacksmithing was beneath him; that he had it in him to build bridges but had never been given the chance.

'Can't waste time,' he said, pushing his empty plate away before Isabel and her uncle had finished eating. 'Where's the machine?'

His confidence at his commission evaporated when he found out that Galbraith had lost the magazine containing the crucial picture of the finished article. 'I shall require my boy Albert,' he announced.

'I can help,' said Isabel.

The blacksmith glanced at Galbraith, then back at Isabel. 'You can help, miss, by summoning my boy Albert.'

Albert happened to live close by. Galbraith went himself, leaving Isabel to supply the mutton sandwich that Jolly had now decided was necessary to undertake the job.

'Ah, Albert,' he said. 'Glad you could join us.'

Albert had seen a photograph and understood much better than his employer how the pieces fitted together. Slowly the machine began to take shape. At a quarter to eleven, after a fierce struggle with the chain, Galbraith proposed they finish for the night. But the blacksmith, fortified by half a bottle of medicinal brandy, had got the bit between his teeth and refused to be separated from his spanner.

By now both wheels were on. A few decisive blows with the hammer fixed the pedals. At half past midnight, as John Bax the lamplighter tottered home and the Chinese baker in Bathurst Road was stoking his oven, the three of them stepped back to admire their handiwork, finished but for a few orphaned nuts and washers and a bolt that wouldn't fit.

It was black, about eight feet long, with a hard leather saddle mounted on two steel springs and handlebars like the horns of an ox. The spoked wheels—the front fractionally larger than the rear—had solid rubber tyres but no brakes. Its diagonal drop-forged frame was inscribed with the flamboyant signature of its inventor, Joshua Holsworthy.

'What's one of these called again?' asked Jolly.

'It's a bicycle,' replied Dr Galbraith.

'A bi-sickel?'

'From the Greek.'

'No doubt.' The blacksmith grunted and dragged his massive forearm across his brow. 'What does it do?'

'I suppose you'd call it a vehicle.'

'A ve-hickel,' said Jolly. He walked around it, crouching now and then to tap it with his spanner. 'From the Greek?'

'Latin.'

'Uh-huh. You ever seen one of these things, Albert?'

Albert saw what answer was required and shook his head.

'And what,' said the blacksmith, 'would be the purpose of this ve-hickel?'

Dr Galbraith did not have a ready answer. According to the advertisement it could cover several miles of firm, level ground at something approaching a brisk walking pace. It was not recommended for use in sand or mud. It carried nothing except its own rider and, judging by its weight, would require two men to heave it aboard an omnibus. 'You know, Jolly,' he said, 'I'm damned if it's got a sensible purpose. But you've got to admit it's a clever piece of work.'

The blacksmith looked at his apprentice. 'What do you think, Albert? Would you fork out twenty quid for one of these bi-sickles?'

The thought of having twenty quid to fork out on anything was so fantastical to Albert that he was lost for an answer. He thrust his hands in his pockets and looked for deliverance to the sarcastic wit of Mr Jolly.

'Of course you wouldn't, lad. Be like…'

Albert held his breath.

'Be like feeding sovereigns to a pig.'

'You've been very helpful, Jolly,' said the doctor, reaching for his purse. 'Let me...'

The blacksmith trousered the note in a flash. 'Experience for the boy,' he said. 'Can't say it'll do him any good, but.' He threw the spanner in his bag. 'Dare say that bloody bi-sickle won't need shoeing, eh, Albert?'

⁓

'Damn beast's got colic,' said O'Hare in the stables of Macy's Hotel. One of the grey geldings had its head sunk in a bag of oats. The other was lying on its side in the straw making a gurgling noise. 'I should cut its windpipe right now. Be better off walking, we would.'

He and Miles had spent three days trotting around Emu Plains and O'Hare was ready to move on. It was a fair guess that every citizen who could read had now been advised of the virtues of Horatio's Boomerang Brandy. O'Hare had done some evangelising of his own in the bar of Macy's Hotel. He considered his job finished. With a clear blue sky beckoning from the south he was looking forward to a week or two among the fertile paddocks of the Nepean Valley before setting their sights on Liverpool, the Georges River and home.

'She'll be right in a couple of days,' said Miles. 'What's the hurry?' It suited him to stay put for a while. Macy's was a dingy sort of hotel but the landlord was friendly, the food was all right and he and O'Hare pretty much had the run of the place. While O'Hare drank in the bar downstairs, Miles sat on the verandah with his feet on the wooden rail, musing. What he wanted was to make a box kite. He could take a foot or two of canvas from the roller and O'Hare wouldn't miss it.

'Horse doctor, are you?' said O'Hare. 'Then perhaps you'll do me the honour of sticking a hand up its backside next time it needs doing?'

'It was just a thought,' said Miles.

O'Hare had been in a truculent mood since the previous night, or rather since dusk, when he'd seen something in the paddock behind the hotel that had disturbed him. What it was he wouldn't say. Now he picked up a handful of straw and rubbed it between his palms and walked out. Miles didn't follow immediately. The sick horse seemed to perk up in O'Hare's absence. Its partner carried on slobbering in its nosebag.

Suddenly Miles heard a cry: 'Jesus bloody wept!' He rushed out to see O'Hare staring off into the paddock. His right hand was trembling. He looked as if he'd seen a ghost. 'There,' he said, 'there's another of the bastards.'

The morning sun was low and bright. Miles had difficulty looking into it.

'Over there,' shouted O'Hare.

Now he saw it, an animal about the size of a cat, with a short white tail, scuttling along a path before diving out of sight.

'Rabbits.'

'So?' replied Miles.

A great weight of sorrow seemed to press down on the older man, who reached out to steady himself on a fence post. He stood for several minutes. At last he said, 'I haven't been flogging brandy all me life, lad. In the beginning I ran sheep, hundreds of 'em. Fine country it was, up in the hills near Geelong. I'd have done all right if it weren't for Sheridan.'

'Thomas?' asked Miles. 'The bloke you pulled out of the lake?'

'That's him. Not that he ever thanked me for it. Never seen such a one for sucking up to a uniform. Governor bloody this and governor bloody that it was. Always taking 'em out shooting. Kangaroos weren't good enough for that lot. Had to be game. Couldn't afford deer and the bloody pheasants wouldn't lay so Sheridan gets his hands on some rabbits and sets 'em loose in the hills. In two years there's so many rabbits a man can't walk a hundred yards from his own back door without losing his bloody foot down a hole. One day a squatter says to me, "The bloke that can wipe these buggers out is going to make himself a rich man."' A long pause followed as O'Hare remembered his fateful decision. 'That,' he said slowly, 'was when I got into the rabbiting game.'

His left arm was tired from leaning on the fence post and he switched to the right. 'For two years I dug and burnt and blasted me way around those hills but the damn rabbits couldn't be stopped, so I sold up and left. When I get to Ballarat I find the rabbits are there already. I've hardly set foot in the Mallee scrub when I'm staring down a bloody warren as wide as a Sydney sewer. By the time I get to the Wimmera the hills are swarming with 'em. They beat me to Swan Hill and at Hay they're camped on both sides of the Murrumbidgee. By now I'm at me wits' end. I'm dreaming of the day I'll bash Thomas Sheridan's skull in with me shovel but a bloke tells me Sheridan's dead from gout and buried in a burrow. "Go north," he says. "I've never seen rabbits above the Lachlan River." So I head north and when I get across the Lachlan there are fifty rabbits grinning at me on the other side. No more, I tell meself, the bastards have beaten me. I throw me gun in the river and climb on a coach to Sydney—'

'But Sydney's full of rabbits,' Miles interrupted.

'They'd been breeding there for forty years,' said O'Hare. 'I had a few quid left and drank the lot. I talked meself into a bed at the Sailors' Home and that was where I heard an old sealer say he'd never heard of rabbits in New Zealand and I reckoned if that was true I'd get some peace at last. So I made up me mind to go.'

Telling his story seemed to have calmed him. O'Hare fumbled for his tobacco pouch and rolled himself an emaciated cigarette. 'I know what you're thinking,' he said. 'You're thinking, how does a man get himself hung up on such a pitiful thing as a rabbit and twist himself into knots trying to get the better of it. Well, a bloke can't always help what gets under his skin and into his brain, and I reckon you'd know that as well as anyone.'

It was a baited line and Miles refused to take it. 'Then you saved Sheridan's life—'

'So he could make mine a bloody misery.'

Miles waited for him to light his cigarette. 'How did it end?' he asked.

O'Hare sucked deeply before resuming his story. Soon after landing at Dunedin, he said, he set out for the Otago goldfields with the aim of supplying provisions to the miners. His experience skinning rabbits had left him with some skills as a barber which he could always put to use. He was keen to get started. The weather was terrible; the sun hadn't shone for weeks. But he noticed familiar faces among the tents and bark-roofed shacks: tough old diggers who'd failed to make their fortunes at Ballarat and Castlemaine. O'Hare pitched in and hoped for the best.

'I was having a feed,' he said, 'with two blokes I'd run into years back on the Murrumbidgee. Ridley and Murchison, I'll never forget 'em if I live to a hundred. It was Murchison did the cooking. "Mutton casserole," he says, throwing a funny look at his mate. "Ridley here found some prime mutton wandering about." Right away I reckoned the stuff was stolen but a feed's a feed and I hadn't eaten all day so I wasn't going to ask to see the butcher's bill. But the pair of 'em keep glancing at each other. Says Murchison, "Got a bit of a taste for the local mutton, haven't we, Ridley?" and the bugger Ridley grins back and I'm still waiting to see the lid come off. "What, no claret?" says Ridley. "What's the place coming to?" Murchison pulls out a flask of rotgut and says do I want a swig. "Never mind the liquor, lads," I say, "just ladle me up a plate of that casserole." So Ridley takes the flask off him and says, "The man's starving, Murchison. Feed him for godsake." Now I'm starting to wonder if there's anything in the pot after all or if these devils are just taking me for a ride. But out it comes and by God it looks the business. "You'll never see a better cook than Murchison here," says Ridley. "Fry up the effin' tailings, he would, and make a meal of 'em." So the two of 'em sit there and watch. "Ain't you hungry, boys?" I say, not wanting to be rude. "Go on," said Ridley, "there's no standing on ceremony here.'"

O'Hare had been ignoring his cigarette, which was now half-burnt. He gazed at the glowing tip. 'As soon as I got a taste of it I knew. I'd have recognised that flesh even if it had been burnt to a cinder. I watched those two buggers smirking but I was that hungry I couldn't stop myself.'

'It was rabbit stew,' said Miles.

'It bloody near finished me off,' said O'Hare. 'I fled the place with nothing but the clothes on me back. Thought of stowin' away to South America but couldn't speak a word of Spanish and was too old to learn. So I wound up back in Sydney and that's how you found me, lad, pushing a cart for a living, with a horse that won't shit when it ought to.'

They sat for a long time in silence. O'Hare's anger had gone out of him. He finished his cigarette and rolled another. Miles wondered whether the story had been told for his benefit. Finally the older man stood up. He was staring at the paddock but his gaze seemed to wander all the way back to the hills around Geelong. 'I told you,' he said, 'all about that bugger Sheridan and what he got up to with his kite, and I wish to God I hadn't. You've had your nose stuck in that notebook like a horse with its head in a bucket. By God almighty, lad, a damn fool that drank himself to death in a silk balloon is no sort of example for a boy like you, and I ain't much of a philosophiser what with rabbits on the brain, but when you're stuck here at the arse end of the world and the country being burrowed out from under you it's fences that's wanted not bloody flying machines.'

⁓

The huge black English safety bicycle stood on a Turkish rug on the floor of Dr Galbraith's study. The steel handlebars gleamed and the leather saddle was buffed with beeswax. It was Tuesday morning. Galbraith had eaten breakfast and spent half an hour climbing on and off the machine with the help of a foot stool. He had become practised at it and could sit plausibly on the saddle with a leg on either side of its diagonal frame. But, however he arranged himself, his feet could not reach the pedals. On first seeing the bicycle he had had his suspicions, which were now confirmed. Whoever was to ride his new toy, it wouldn't be him.

He was perched there in his blue serge suit when Isabel walked in. She sized the situation up. Her first words were, 'It'll take a giant to ride it.'

'Or an orang-utan,' said her uncle. 'Help me off, will you?'

Galbraith bent down to admire the oily combination of cranks and cogs by which Holsworthy's machine converted the up-and-down movement of the legs into circular motion of the chain wheel. It was like peering inside the workings of a pocket watch. 'Tell me, Isabel,' he said, 'do you think Mr Holsworthy's bicycle will ever catch on?'

'Not if he insists on painting it black,' she answered.

The doctor scratched his chin. His niece's way of thinking never failed to intrigue him. The colour seemed to him of no significance at all.

'It would catch on much quicker,' she said, 'if he painted it gold.' She put both hands on his shoulders and moved him out of the way. 'Now let me have a go.'

But Isabel could reach the pedals only by standing out of the saddle.

Galbraith glanced out of the window and happened to see the blacksmith's apprentice walking past with a sack of charcoal on his shoulder. 'I fear our bicycle is useless,' he said, 'unless…'

'Unless what?'

'Young Albert is a strapping lad. I wonder if he can be persuaded.' He opened the french windows and called him over.

'Albert, you're an athletic type,' he said. 'I dare say you could ride this machine if you had to.'

The apprentice was reluctant at first. Jolly had sent him out to fetch the charcoal and would be expecting him back. He wouldn't come more than a step inside the room. Isabel was making him bashful. All the blood in his body rushed to his ears, which glowed like hibiscus flowers.

'Never mind the charcoal, Albert,' said the doctor. 'I have a wheelbarrow. We'll push it along behind you.'

Isabel laughed.

'My niece will push it,' he said.

'No I won't,' said Isabel. 'I'll be with you, Albert.'

Albert folded his muscular arms against his chest, as he always did when he thought someone was making fun of him. The black-smith would pull his leg by proposing tasks he had no intention of letting him do. 'Here, Albert,' he'd say. 'How about knocking up a new rim for this coach wheel? I'll just sit here and watch.' Or 'Never mind that horseshoe, Albert. Make us a nice pair of candlesticks while I have my tea.' The boy searched Galbraith's round face for any sign of a grin. 'S'pose,' he said at last.

'Do you enjoy blacksmithing, Albert?'

'Mostly. Not always. I like the hammer.'

'So I can see,' said the doctor, admiring his left bicep. 'Left-handed, I'll wager.'

Albert cocked his head suspiciously. Hammering, to his way of thinking, was a serious business, not something to be wagered on, especially by men in blue suits. Though bludgeoned daily on the anvil of Mr Jolly's sparkling wit, Albert was far from stupid. But he was shy, especially in the presence of females younger than his mother, and his ears were large.

Galbraith sensed his mistake. 'A quarter of an hour, Albert, and Mr Jolly will have his charcoal.'

'All right,' said Albert.

'Good lad.' He doubted that any of the pound note he had given the blacksmith had found its way to his apprentice. 'For your help last night,' he said, chinking a pair of half-crowns into his hand. Albert turned to Isabel and blushed again.

In the twenty-four hours since O'Hare had told his life story a great change had come over him. Now he was shaved as smooth as a river pebble. His variegated suit was brushed clean and his black felt hat was as good as new. A burden had been lifted off him. After having one of the horses shod, he'd spent Monday afternoon in sympathetic conversation with the widowed owner of the Emu Plains Butter Factory and hadn't returned to his room until the early hours of Tuesday morning. At the crack of dawn he set off with his one good horse to deliver his slogans to some of the farms scattered around the outskirts of town.

In the light of this transformation, Miles borrowed a pair of scissors and helped himself to a yard and a half of canvas from the roller. He bought a dozen dowelling rods, a roll of twine and some strong thread from a household goods supplier and built himself a canvas box kite.

He carried it out to the paddock behind Macy's hotel. The kite was heavy, much heavier than he'd expected. It seemed too cumbersome to fly. But the wind had picked up and, by extending the length of twine and running into the wind, instead of ahead of it, he had seen the kite leap ten feet into the air. Miles mastered the art of keeping it airborne, and now the word BOOMERANG rippled and flapped twenty-five feet above his head. This, he knew intuitively, was the basis for his flying machine. On the ground it was as squat as a tea chest, but once aloft it dipped and soared like a swallow. He felt it tugging his arm and realised the strength behind it. The gliders he'd built seemed puny by comparison.

His stitching, however, was barely up to the task. The kite landed heavily. When Miles went to pick it up he found one of the dowelling rods hanging by a thread. The frame wanted reinforcing and for that he needed more twine.

Miles was striding down the main street when he saw Albert hurtling towards him on the bicycle. He had seen one on the pier at Manly. The boy could barely control where he was going and veered from one side of the street to the other. Dust billowed from the wheels. Chasing after it was a girl of eighteen or twenty in a bright yellow dress. A stout figure in a blue serge suit followed a long way behind, pushing a wheelbarrow. The girl herself seemed almost airborne in the dust. Masses of tangled hair flew over her shoulders. She had thrown off her hat, which was rolling on the street. The bicycle was getting away from her. Miles was transfixed by the girl as the machine swerved towards him and they were both shouting and a second later he was lying on his back in the dirt. There was an unnatural kink between his wrist and elbow.

A small crowd swarmed around him, less excited by Miles's injuries than by the machine that had caused them.

'Oh my God,' cried Isabel, crouching over him, 'are you all right?'

Albert was already getting up. He was dazed and bruised but otherwise unhurt. He wandered about unsteadily as Dr Galbraith, having abandoned the wheelbarrow, stumbled to his aid. 'Are you injured, lad?' At that moment the crowd peeled apart and he saw Miles lying there with his niece beside him.

'Get away, get away,' he said, elbowing his way through. 'Are you hurt, lad?' He knelt down and saw that Miles's arm was broken. 'Easy, lad, don't move.'

Galbraith reached for his bag and realised he didn't have it. He looked down the street at the two red lamps indicating the neighbouring surgeries of Sproule and L'Estrange. 'Someone fetch L'Estrange,' he said. 'Tell him to bring chloroform.'

'Is it very painful?' asked Isabel. Miles attempted to shake his head. He was pale from shock.

As they waited for L'Estrange, a burly figure in leather braces and shirt sleeves pushed his way to the front. Seeing the bewildered look on his apprentice's face, he clicked his tongue and said, 'That there, young Albert, is what you get for riding a bi-sickel.'

Albert was too embarrassed to argue. He glanced about for the missing sack of charcoal.

'A bi-sickel, ladies and gentlemen,' continued Jolly. 'From the Greek.'

The blacksmith hooked his thumbs under his braces and rocked on his heels. Had he carried in his pocket a horseshoe, or some other example of his blacksmithing talents, he would have taken it out and passed it around. There was no silencing him.

'I said when I saw it, ladies and gentlemen, I said "That bi-sickel is a dangerous machine." I warned young Albert there, but would he listen? Thank heavens the boy isn't dead, though it'd serve him right if he was, what with the riot he's caused.'

Jolly hadn't noticed Miles lying on the ground. His scorn was directed publicly at Albert, but implicitly at Dr Galbraith. Miles's fractured arm lay across his chest. He was feeling nauseous.

Jolly hadn't finished. Looking around, his eye fell on an elderly Chinese whom he had once found standing outside his gate with a broken rake. 'As if it ain't bad enough,' he went on, 'to have bi-sickels running amok on the streets, and pigtails waiting to strangle us in our beds, and all our gold shipped off to China.'

Galbraith glanced over his shoulder. 'Would that we all had your perspicacity, Mr Jolly,' he said. 'This town would be a great deal safer.'

The blacksmith took this as a compliment. He cast around for a suitable note to finish on but all he could manage was, 'Well, that's all right then.' He looked for Albert, who was hovering in the background. 'Now, Albert,' he said, 'where's that blasted charcoal?'

'It's my fault,' said Isabel. 'I made Albert go faster.'

Miles's eyes rolled back in their sockets, trying to see her more clearly.

'It was an accident,' said Galbraith, cross with himself for being the cause of it. He looked up and saw Dr L'Estrange brushing some dust off his lapel. The physicians shook hands coolly. 'Be a good fellow L'Estrange, and give the boy some chloroform. He's in more pain than he lets on.' He turned to Miles. 'What is your name, young man? Never mind, it doesn't matter. My colleague here will give you something to ease the pain and I shall take you home to fix your arm.'

L'Estrange handed him the bottle. He could see it was an ugly break and did not want to be implicated in mending it.

Galbraith shook a small amount of the colourless liquid onto a handkerchief. Miles recognised the odour at once. He had a vision of Wolunsky's cape. Isabel was bending over him. He could feel her long hair on his forehead. As he inhaled the sickly scent, his eyelids grew heavy and he felt himself floating again.

~

'I've been wondering when you'd wake,' said Isabel. 'You were miles away.' She'd been staring at him for some time. She liked the length of him, the thin face and angular cheekbones. He reminded her of one of those long medieval knights she'd seen in books, lying in effigy on his tomb with a faithful dog curled up at his feet.

'Where am I?' asked Miles.

He was in a bed he'd never seen before, in pyjamas that didn't fit, in a house he'd never visited. It was dark outside and a thin crescent moon was showing through the curtains. There was a dull pain in his arm, which was plastered and resting on a table beside him.

'You broke your arm, that is we broke it, Albert knocked you over and my uncle mended it.' Isabel paused. 'He's very good with bones.'

Miles took in the room, the macabre furniture, the tea chest overflowing with magazines, and the green-eyed girl who was sitting in a large red armchair by the window. 'So where am I?'

'In my uncle's house. We tracked down your friend Mr O'Hare. He didn't think you'd mind.' She shut the book she'd been reading. 'Do you mind?'

'No.'

She was wearing a man's woollen dressing gown that was too short for her, leaving her calves bare, and a pair of leather slippers that presumably belonged to the same person. 'Does it hurt?' she asked.

'Yes,' he answered.

'It looked gruesome. It probably felt worse.'

'It did.'

'It was a nasty break but he's confident it will heal properly...he's very good with bones.'

'So you keep saying.'

Isabel scowled. She'd expected him to be more gracious. 'Have I said it before?'

'Twice,' said Miles. 'Maybe three times.'

'Oh.' She shrugged. 'Your name is Miles?'

He guessed O'Hare had told her. 'And yours?'

'Isabel. This is my uncle's house. I come here quite often. I live in Sydney.'

Miles hauled himself up in bed, hoping she might offer to help, but Isabel stayed where she was. 'That machine...' he began.

'An English safety bicycle,' said Isabel. 'Not very safe, it turns out.'

'Yours?'

Isabel realised she'd been staring. She had noticed something familiar about him while he slept. She didn't want to betray her interest by asking him directly, not until she knew more. 'My uncle's,' she said. 'I helped put it together.'

'Really?'

'Well, I sort of helped. I watched anyway.' She looked out of the window at the damaged bicycle which the doctor had paid five shillings to have brought back in a cart and dumped in the shed with his buggy.

'I've seen one before,' said Miles, 'on Manly pier.'

'You know Sydney?'

'I've been there a few times.' He noticed Smith's notebook in her lap. 'Isn't that—'

'Oh, I'm sorry. It fell out of your pocket. I didn't mean...that is, I was looking after it.' In slapping the book shut she accidentally dropped it. She bent to pick it up. 'Is it yours? Did you write it?'

'It's mine,' said Miles, 'and I didn't write it.'

'Who did?'

He had any number of reasons for not telling her, or not telling her now. He wanted to know more about her first. He was annoyed with her for having the book at all.

'Who wrote it?' asked Isabel.

'Tobias Smith.'

She sat up straight. 'The balloonist?'

Miles resisted the urge to open the book and check all the pages were there. He put it down on the table beside the bed. 'You've heard of him?'

'More than that,' she said. 'I stood in his basket!'

He didn't believe her and said so.

'Years ago,' she said. 'Hyde Park. I was seven…I climbed in the basket—don't ask me how—and it took off. It was in all the papers. Of course, I never saw him again. He's dead now.'

'I know,' said Miles.

'Quite a dreamer, wasn't he? Mr Smith, I mean.'

'Was he?'

She found Miles's answers irritating. 'You should know. Your friend Mr O'Hare warned us. "Don't lose that bloody book," he said, "or there'll be trouble." The bit I read was gibberish. It was like the ramblings of a lunatic.'

'What would you know about it? You had no right to pry.'

'I wasn't prying,' said Isabel.

'What would you call it?'

Isabel stood up and pulled the cord around her dressing gown. 'Good night, Miles. I hope you sleep well. I really am very sorry about your accident.'

Isabel wasn't accustomed to having men of her own age speak back to her. Usually they fawned, if not on her then on her mother. Miles had been brusque, even rude. She couldn't imagine him ever fawning. She found that attractive.

It was before seven when she came downstairs. She was surprised to find the front door open and her uncle wandering in from the shed. There was frost on the lawn and his short dainty strides were visible in the sun.

'No sign of the patient?' he asked.

'Sound asleep,' she answered. 'Isn't it a bit early to be gardening?'

Isabel was wearing thick cotton knickerbockers, dark grey and gathered in at the knee; a plain blouse of a colour her uncle would have described as blue but was in truth a delicate lilac; and black ankle boots, laced up the front. Galbraith considered her outfit with a mix of curiosity and amusement. He thought of asking if the lower garment had a name but decided it could wait. 'I wasn't gardening,' he said. 'I was having a look at Mr Holsworthy's bicycle. I think it is not beyond repair. In fact the damage appears quite minimal. Our friend upstairs got much the worst of it.'

'He's rather surly,' said Isabel.

'Is he? I was under the impression you'd taken a liking to him. You sat in his room for long enough.' He bent down to remove his shoes but saw that his slippers were missing. 'Or was that,' he added, 'in your office as nurse?'

'I didn't say I disliked him. I just said he was surly.'

'He was probably in a good deal of pain.'

'He didn't want me reading his notebook.'

'I don't think I'd want you reading my notebook,' said Galbraith.

'I didn't know you had one.'

'I don't, dear.'

Isabel frowned and shut the door. 'I probably should have asked him.'

'Probably.'

She smelt kippers and followed her uncle into the dining room, where a silver poacher was simmering over a little oil heater.

'I thought you might want to take him breakfast,' said the doctor. 'He may not take it, of course, now that you've offended him.'

'I'll risk it,' she said.

~

'Hello,' Isabel remarked coolly.

Miles pulled himself up with difficulty. He felt ridiculous in the doctor's pyjamas.

'Does it hurt?' she asked.

'Less than it did.'

Isabel had the legs for knickerbockers, especially dark-grey ones, which set off her slender hips and pearly skin. When she'd worn them on the promenade at Coogee beach, passers-by forgot what they were saying and stared. She put the tray down on the table next to the bed and drew back the curtains.

'What do you call those?' he asked, pointing at the knicker-bockers.

'I could ask you the same thing,' she said, indicating his pyjamas.

He thought for a while before saying, 'They suit you.'

144

'Thanks,' replied Isabel. 'I'm afraid yours don't.' She sat down in the red armchair and crossed her legs. 'Aren't you going to eat the breakfast I brought you?'

He hadn't eaten anything since the previous morning. The chloroform had made him nauseous. Now the sickly aftertaste had worn off and he was starving. He ate quickly while Isabel stared out the window, asking innocuous questions that Miles was content to answer with a nod or a shake of the head. Once or twice she mentioned Tobias Smith in the hope of prising out of him the story of the leatherbound notebook. But Dr Galbraith's pianola was playing loudly downstairs and Miles either pretended not to hear or changed the subject. Isabel smiled at his evasions. They were so artless. She would have to be patient.

⁓

Miles felt awkward in the house and wanted to leave, but Galbraith wouldn't hear of it.

'Where would you go, young man? Macy's Hotel?'

'I've slept in worse,' said Miles. He knew that O'Hare would still be there.

'I don't doubt it,' replied the doctor. 'I've slept in worse myself. In fact I've spent some agreeable evenings in Macy's. But this is a medical opinion, not a social one. The bone needs time to knit and, until I'm certain it's knitting as it should, I insist on your staying in this house.'

'I'd have to work. I won't be fed for nothing.'

'Who says you'll be fed at all, Miles? I have a gardener so old he is moribund. Your one arm is more useful than his two. Your eating will depend on your willingness to tame the wisteria.'

'I reckon I could do that,' said Miles.

'There is, of course, my niece Isabel to consider. She's rather a handful for a man of my antique habits. Your being here would probably be a diversion for her.'

'A diversion from what?' asked Miles. As far as he could see, Isabel didn't do anything except drink her uncle's sherry, go on long walks by herself and read books that didn't belong to her.

'From talking to me for one thing,' said Galbraith.

'She's avoiding me anyway.' Miles had intended this to be matter-of-fact but it sounded petulant.

'Is she really? That's surprising. But the mind of a young woman was never one to be penetrated by the likes of us.'

Miles looked away.

'The fact remains,' said Galbraith, 'I intend you to remain here for no less than a fortnight. After that I shall be happy to release you.' He seemed to be hunting for a letter among the various books and journals that littered the house. Miles followed him as he opened drawers and shuffled papers. 'By the way, Isabel tells me that you are practical, by which she means more practical than I am, which is not an extravagant compliment.' Finally Galbraith found what he was looking for: a large stiff brown envelope that rattled when he picked it up. Inside was an assortment of nuts, bolts and washers 'left over' after Albert and Mr Jolly had finished assembling the bicycle. 'I'm more inclined to blame the workmen than the machine,' he said.

'Let me have them,' said Miles.

'Why?'

'You want the bicycle mended, don't you?'

'I should have thought you'd never want to see it again.'

An image flashed through Miles's head of Isabel flying after

Albert in a cloud of dust. 'I hardly saw it the first time,' he said. 'No,' muttered the doctor. 'I don't expect you did.'.

≈⌒

There is more than one way to read a story. And more than one way to look at a bicycle. When Joshua Holsworthy of High Street, Taunton, contemplated his English safety bicycle he saw the middle classes putting clips on their trouser legs and hitching up their skirts and riding into the countryside on Sunday afternoons. He saw cycling clubs multiplying like amoeba, races with foreigners, export opportunities to the United States of America.

Sometimes, during a slap-up lunch with his backers, he imagined lucrative orders from sedentary generals convinced it was cheaper to oil a bicycle than feed and water a horse. He pictured a world that might one day be persuaded to abandon walking and entrust all its social, sporting and recreational needs to the double-sprung beeswaxed comfort of an English safety bicycle.

When Miles gazed at the bicycle he saw a machine that reminded him of the grinding cogs and squealing gears that shuddered away below the revolving stage of the Prince of Wales Theatre. As a boy, he'd watched in awe as the big black engine made by Gould & Sons of Bolton, Lancashire, thundered into life. He loved nothing more than to lie face down in the flies staring at the stage rotating beneath him. When Eliza grounded him, he would sneak underneath, where Mr Govett with an oily rag around his palm adjusted the valves and hammered faulty pistons with a wooden mallet. Looking at the bicycle's brass pedals and spinning cranks, he could see the two machines had a lot in common. If you imagined the rider's legs as pistons, the main cog was the drive shaft. Both fed a revolving cylinder. In short, the English safety bicycle was an engine just like those made by Gould & Sons of Bolton, Lancashire, only it was a fraction of the weight.

'Here you are,' said Isabel, standing in the doorway of the stables. Miles couldn't tell how long she'd been there. She was leaning with her arms folded, silhouetted against the bright winter sky. 'Think you can repair it?' she asked.

'It's not broken,' said Miles. 'Just bent out of shape.'

The front wheel was warped and the handlebars had been knocked sideways. One of the pedals was crooked. 'Of course,' he added, holding up the brown envelope, 'there are a few pieces I've got to find a home for. It'll probably be easier to pull the whole thing apart and start again.'

'You've only got one arm,' Isabel reminded him.

'You could help. Unless you've got something better to do.'

'It can wait,' she said. 'Won't we need tools?'

'A spanner. A pair of pliers.'

'Stay here,' said Isabel. She returned ten minutes later with an assortment of tools, none of which had ever been used. She was red in the face. Galbraith was out visiting patients. There was just the pair of them.

Joshua Holsworthy's bicycle was ingeniously simple. With no brakes and no gears it didn't take long to dismantle it and put it together as its maker intended.

Isabel held while Miles tightened. Sometimes they swapped over. He was right-handed, she was left. In two hours they had it finished. Isabel was convinced now she'd seen him before. 'I know who you are,' she said. 'The levitator. He called for a volunteer. It was you.'

Miles borrowed a smile he had seen Wolunsky use when he wanted to give the impression he was not who someone thought he was.

'It was you, wasn't it?'

'It could have been.'

Isabel was all for games but only if she had all the cards. 'Was it or wasn't it?' she demanded.

'Yes.'

She hooked her hands behind her head. 'I knew it. Now tell me his secret.'

'His secret?' he asked. 'Or mine?'

'Very funny. You're not going to tell me you were born to be levitated?' She looked away and when she looked back the same smile had reappeared on his face. 'Or are you?'

'It's an acquired skill,' he said. 'I acquired it early.'

'You're pulling my leg, Miles.'

'Am I?'

'Put the bicycle down,' said Isabel. 'Sit exactly where you are and tell me everything.'

Miles didn't tell her everything. He didn't even tell her half of it. But he told her enough about his life with Eliza and Wolunsky, edited and embroidered as he saw fit, to hold Isabel's attention.

For once she didn't interrupt, though she raised her eyebrows a couple of times. There had been something about him from the start that interested her. He was not like other young men she had met or was likely to meet. He was spirited, quick-tempered, evasive. His hair needed cutting; he reminded her of a sculptor's work-in-progress. He appeared to have no dress sense at all; the last time she'd seen Geelong tweed trousers and a beaver overcoat

on the same person was in a pantomime when she was twelve.
'Your father,' she said at last. 'You haven't mentioned him.'
Miles hesitated. 'He's dead,' he said.

Miles had not forgotten O'Hare, and vice versa. The sense of
obligation was mostly on Miles's side; the sense of injury on
the other.

'The point is this,' said O'Hare. They were sitting over pints
of dark ale at the bar of Macy's Hotel. Apart from the barman,
who was dozing on his stool, the place was deserted. 'The point
is, I'm not bothered about the loss of it, only what if Mr Horatio
gets to measuring his property and comes up short? That, lad, is
what you might call an invidious situation and one a man
wouldn't want to find himself in if he could help it.'

Miles nodded and sipped his beer. O'Hare had spent the past
hour making him feel guilty for having taken the canvas for his
box kite. Not that he felt the loss personally. One slogan less didn't
matter to him. But he reckoned that Miles intended to leave and
was doing his best to stop him. Miles held up his plastered arm
but the older man waved it away. It was quite possible for him to
turn the crank with his other arm and in any case, O'Hare added
quickly, it was the company he was after.

'What I mean is, who's to say a stranger didn't nick it while
me back was turned? That'd look like negligence, wouldn't it? A
man could wind up in court with a charge like that around his
neck. I'd need someone to back me up, wouldn't I, and that'd be
you, lad.'

Sitting on the counter between them was the yard and a half

in question, rolled by O'Hare into a tight bundle containing the twelve dowelling rods Miles had used to build his box kite. O'Hare, it was clear, had gone to some trouble to unpick the stitching and remove any suggestion that the structure had ever been capable of flying.

'I'll tell you what. We'll follow the river for a few days, see how it grabs us. Head for Liverpool if we don't like it. Back in Pitt Street in a fortnight. How does that sound?'

It sounded to Miles exactly like the plan O'Hare had been proposing before the horse got sick.

'It's that girl, isn't it?' said O'Hare, lifting his glass and tipping back the contents. 'I knew it.'

The barman put down a couple more pints.

'And if it ain't her,' he went on, 'it's that bloody doctor with his machines.'

'He wants a gardener,' said Miles.

O'Hare slapped his beer on the counter. 'A gardener?' he replied, trying not to laugh.

'Why not?' asked Miles.

'A one-armed bloody gardener?'

Miles sucked the froth off his new pint. 'I'm on half pay,' he said. He didn't volunteer any more and O'Hare, in any case, didn't want to hear it. The truth was Miles wanted to stay because he didn't want to go. It wasn't Isabel or the bicycle or the box kite that was keeping him, but all three. Fate had thrown possibilities in his way and Miles was not ready to desert them.

'Keep your feet on the ground, lad,' said O'Hare, 'that's my advice.'

'I'll remember that,' answered Miles.

O'Hare lit a cigarette and finished his drink in silence. He stayed for a day or two, touching up his slogans with a tin of black paint, then hitched the horses to his cart and informed the landlord he was going. Miles never saw him—or the canvas—again.

⌒

In September 1852 Francois Perigord's manned dirigible flew seventeen miles with the aid of a three-horsepower steam engine attached to a wooden propeller. The cotton envelope was 144 feet long and filled with coal gas and the dirigible flew at an average speed of five miles per hour. There was a small engraving of Perigord's craft in the lobby of the Mechanics' Institute in Sydney. Miles had often stood in front of it on his visits to the reading room, trying to guess the weight of such a load and the wingspan that would be needed to lift it. He was reminded of it now by the incessant rattle from the nearby flour mill, where a second-hand steam engine had been installed to replace the old windmill.

It had rained all morning and Isabel was off on one of her solitary walks. Miles seized the opportunity of being alone to flout the doctor's orders by riding the bicycle. Trundling one-handed among the flowerbeds, he realised just how efficient it was. The machine was cumbersome, yet the relative sizes of the cogs meant the rider could propel it with a minimum of effort. Miles thought back to a page in the notebook in which Smith had drawn a glider shaped like a crucifix, with the arms formed out of box kites. Suddenly it dawned on him: why not use Holsworthy's pedal-and-chain mechanism to propel Smith's glider?

Miles rolled to a halt beside the metal arch on the front lawn. He was tired and the bicycle was unsteady. It was a struggle to dismount without falling over. The light was starting to fade and it was raining again.

'It looks like you've been going round in circles,' Isabel said from under her umbrella.

Miles glanced down and saw his figure-of-eight track engraved on the wet grass. 'Not exactly,' he said.

She helped him wheel the bicycle back inside the stables. 'I've been doing some thinking, Miles.'

'Have you?'

Isabel shook the rain off her umbrella and dropped it in a pot outside the front door. 'I want to be levitated. I want you to levitate me.'

'That's ridiculous,' Miles replied. He stood dripping on the doctor's rug. He thought she was making fun of him. There was a letter on the mantelpiece but Miles saw it wasn't for him. 'I've been levitated,' he said. 'I've never done it to anyone.'

'But you know how.'

'No,' he said.

'No what? No, you won't; or no, you don't know how?'

'No, I won't.'

'Spoilsport,' she said.

Miles glared at her. She hadn't worn a hat and the rain had slanted under her umbrella. Her wet hair glistened. There was a suggestion of a pout on her lips. Now he was tempted.

'You're thinking about it,' said Isabel.

'No.'

Halfway up the stairs the winter sun gave a brittle luminescence to the window. There was a small landing beneath it, where the staircase turned back on itself. Isabel saw him looking at it. 'Do it there, under the window. I want a halo around me.' She grabbed his good hand. 'Go on, Miles.'

'It won't work.'

'Then prove it. I won't ask again. And I'll never say a word to anyone.'

Miles felt strangely aroused. A charge seemed to play around his fingers, as it often did before Wolunsky had levitated him. Isabel was still holding his hand. She was conscious of it trembling.

'All right,' he said.

They walked up the staircase, Isabel in front. He still had his plaster on. His other arm ached from riding the bicycle. He took an ivory-handled walking stick from the hook by the door. Of course, he didn't have Wolunsky's brass disc. But Isabel had a pendant around her neck, a Chinese charm made of pink jade that she wore on a gold chain. 'I'll need that,' he said.

She didn't ask why but gave it to him. There was a little cane chair at the top of the stairs that her uncle stood on when he wanted to open the window. Isabel hurried up to fetch it. 'What about you?' she asked. 'Don't you need one?'

Miles shook his head.

'What now?' she asked.

Miles made her sit at an angle to the window. He balanced the walking stick under her left elbow. The deepening sun turned the jade almost scarlet. 'Watch the pendant,' he said.

'I am watching it.'

'And don't talk.'

Miles held the chain still and gave the edge of the pendant a flick with the nail of his middle finger. The jade spun, throwing splinters of light around the walls. Isabel stared at it, trying not to blink. Miles began to speak in a slow, measured monotone. He recited automatically, from memory, the first words that came into his head: 'Let us know our indiscretion sometimes serves us well when our deep plots do pall.'

Isabel paid no attention to the words. Perhaps she didn't even hear them. She was concentrating on the spinning pendant. Miles reached the end of his soliloquy and started again. Isabel's eyelids began, at last, to droop. She was breathing more slowly. Her chest was hardly moving.

Suddenly the walking stick that Miles had balanced under her elbow fell away. Isabel didn't notice, or if she noticed she didn't show it. Miles watched the stick cartwheel down the staircase and come to rest on the rug. He was sure he had seen her elbow move, just a fraction, enough to dislodge it. Without the stick her arm flopped by her side. Isabel's eyes were shut. Her mouth was slightly open. Miles could feel her breath on the back of his hand.

He moved behind her and grasped the chair. It seemed to slide away from under her, an inch or two at most. He wasn't sure. He might have imagined it. He breathed her name softly but she didn't respond. Were her feet hovering just above the floor? For a few moments he thought they were, but now he saw they were pressing down firmly on the carpet. She was sitting slightly forward on the chair but maybe she had been from the start. She might have been susceptible for an instant but the instant had gone.

He walked around until he was facing her again. 'Nothing,' he said. 'Sorry.'

'But I felt it,' she said.

'No, you didn't.'

'I felt it. I felt myself floating.'

'I was watching. You didn't move. Or rather you did move but you didn't levitate.'

Miles gave her back the pendant. She snatched it from him and clipped it around her neck. 'I felt it, Miles. Whatever you say, I felt myself floating. You have the power, after all. Why are you denying it?'

'You probably imagined it,' said Miles.

'So tell me what it feels like.'

'What?' He was returning the chair to its place at the top of the stairs. Isabel was still standing by the window.

'Go on, Miles, say what it feels like to be levitated.'

'It's a long time since I did it.'

'It's not something you'd forget.'

Miles looked down the stairs at her. 'It's like being lifted out of your own skin. Your arms and legs belong to someone else.'

'Is that all?' asked Isabel. It sounded almost banal, like being drunk.

Miles remembered that first evening in the Royal Victoria Theatre, feeling his own thoughts unravelling as he listened to the tale of the Sicilian apothecary. Wolunsky's stories, even the most prosaic ones, had the power of spells. 'You'll know if it happens,' he said.

Isabel was convinced she had floated but she knew she would never talk Miles into believing it. He followed her into the doctor's sitting room, where she poured herself a large sherry. She sat down sideways on a green velvet sofa, filling it. Miles took the doctor's leather armchair.

The walls were covered with photographs mounted in heavy black frames, the legacy of one of Galbraith's early mechanical infatuations. The camera was somewhere, together with its tripod and portable darkroom and various flagons containing the remnants of chemicals needed to sensitise the wet plates. The sharp whiff of collodion was still discernible in the laundry. The plates themselves were long dried up, but the images were preserved in dozens of blurry albumen prints. They were mostly of the garden and the mountains, though the doctor had tried his hand at portraits and had once tried unsuccessfully to photograph a horse. The pictures fascinated Isabel. She wanted to take some herself but didn't have the patience to prepare the plates.

'So tell me, Miles, what's all this got to do with your friend Tobias Smith?'

'I knew him. I didn't say he was my friend.'

'But you have his notebook. You were kindred spirits or something.'

'Or something,' said Miles.

Isabel sat for a while nursing her sherry. 'All right,' she said at last, 'don't tell me. I'm sure I wouldn't understand. I think I'd like another sherry. Will you have one?'

'I drink beer.'

'I'll bet you do. But my uncle doesn't. So if you're going to join me you'll just have to acquire a taste for something else.' She walked over to the drinks cabinet. 'Scotch, maybe?'

Miles shrugged. He half expected to be offered Horatio's Boomerang Brandy but was happy to settle for whisky. After the first he said yes to another. It was a Friday evening. On Fridays Dr Galbraith usually found an excuse to stop off for a couple of drinks at the Commercial Hotel or Macy's or the Horse and Jockey. He rarely returned before eight.

· The whisky went to Miles's head. He could hear Wolunsky's voice, a story he'd told in the officers' mess at Newcastle barracks.

'A Portuguese scholar,' Miles began, 'called Hector Jesus Salamanca once saw a tortoise snatched from the ground by an eagle and was convinced the tortoise was the better flier.'

'Perhaps he was drunk,' said Isabel.

Miles ignored her. 'Salamanca,' he went on, 'bought a tortoise from the market for a few escudos and spent weeks following the animal on his hands and knees trying to coax it into flight, or at least make it jump the stream that ran at the bottom of his garden. In the end he realised its short legs were completely unsuited to flying and was kicking himself for his foolishness when it occurred to him to examine the shell. That evening he placed the tortoise upside down on a pond. He saw it float for almost a minute before it became disoriented and sank. From this he reckoned that, if the conditions were right, the shell would float just as well on air. He rushed down to the public library—'

'Where did he live?' asked Isabel.

'Lisbon,' said Miles. 'The city was full of libraries. He went to the biggest.'

'And?'

'He found a book of drawings by Leonardo da Vinci in which he saw a flying machine that resembled a tortoiseshell rotating on a spindle. Salamanca was convinced he was onto something. One day he confided in his neighbour. This bloke made a living writing eulogies and verses—'

'What sort of verses?'

'Romantic verses.'

Isabel looked incredulous. 'Why not bawdy verses? No-one makes a living selling romantic verses.'

'If you say so. Anyway, the man knew nothing about flying. But he'd heard there were certain islands in the Pacific where turtles as big as cartwheels came ashore to lay eggs.

'That was all Salamanca needed to hear. He sold everything he owned and hopped aboard a trading barque bound for Malacca, on the west coast of Malaya. From there he took a ship to Fiji, where (said the neighbour) giant turtles were caught and eaten by the natives.

'When he got there he discovered the turtles had already left for the season. The coolies on the wharves told him he'd have to wait another year. He settled down to wait in a fishing village on the far side of the island where he amused himself watching flying fish skimming over the waves.

'Zoologists have said that Salamanca had pinned his hopes on the wrong turtle. The loggerhead turtle, *Caretta caretta*, is found all over the Pacific but its big hard bony shell was no good to Salamanca. He would have done better hunting the pancake tortoise, *Malacocherus tornieri*, whose shell is flat and flexible.'

'What about his wife?' asked Isabel.

'Who said he had a wife?'

'I can't see Mrs Salamanca accompanying him on his wild goose chase.'

'She didn't,' Miles replied crossly. 'He left her behind. She was much older than he was. She thought the world was flat.'

'It sounds like they were a well-matched couple.' She hung one leg over the arm of the sofa. 'Go on.'

'While waiting for the turtles to return,' said Miles, 'Salamanca wrestled with the problem of how to propel his shell through the air. At first he wanted to row it but after paddling a native canoe out to sea he realised he didn't have the strength. He thought of attaching a pair of bellows but found they were impractical. The same went for a canvas sail. He dabbled with the idea of using pulleys to draw the craft along a fixed rope but realised it would limit the scope of his travels. In the end he decided he had no choice but to hire a pair of natives to paddle it for him.

'Twelve months passed and there was no sign of the turtles. By now he was so convinced of his genius that a year more or less made no difference to him. So he waited another year, drinking and gambling away his savings in the certainty that he'd soon be a rich man, courted by kings and emperors.

'But the turtles didn't return the next year or the year after that. Salamanca began to suspect that his neighbour had sent him to the other side of the world just to get him out of the way so that he could patent the flying machine for himself. He screamed and beat the walls at the realisation that a great scholar had been tricked by a writer of smutty lyrics.'

'Did he blame his wife?' asked Isabel.

'It wasn't her fault.'

'But did he blame her?'

'She was dead of the plague,' said Miles. 'Salamanca had no-one to blame but himself. All his money was gone. Desperate to return home, he begged for a passage from every ship's captain he met but got no further than Singapore. Day after day he sat on the docks staring out to sea until one day he fell in and was never seen again.

'Meanwhile, the neighbour, far from claiming the idea for himself, had made a fortune by writing a comedy about a scholar who thought turtles could fly and spent his life trying to prove it. When, many years later, news reached him of the unhappy end of the man who had given him his story, the neighbour decided to write a sequel, a much darker tale of blighted ambition with none of the erotic passages. This proved even more popular.

Readers wanted to know if such a man had ever existed. They found a dignity in his pursuit of the impossible. They admired his tenacity. They refused to believe that the same man, Hector Jesus Salamanca, could have inspired both stories.'

'It was the same story,' said Isabel, hooking her hands behind her head. 'The difference was all in the telling.'

Miles didn't say anything for a long time. His glass was empty. He wasn't sure yet if he could trust her.

'Tell me,' said Isabel.

'Tell you what?'

'Whatever it is you're thinking of telling me.'

'I'm going to fly,' said Miles.

'Isn't that what you have been doing?'

'I mean real flying. Not spinning discs and hocus pocus.'

'In a balloon?'

'A balloon goes where the wind blows it. What I'm talking about is a machine.'

Isabel sat up, spilling some of her sherry on the sofa. 'You mean the sort that no-one's ever managed to build?'

Miles didn't contradict her.

'What are you saying, Miles? That while the French and Americans are slaving away in their workshops, the answers are all here in Tobias Smith's notebook? Isn't that a bit far-fetched?'

'Where we are is pretty far-fetched. Kangaroos are far-fetched.'

'Do they fly too?' asked Isabel.

Miles stood up.

'Don't go,' said Isabel. 'Convince me.'

'You don't want to hear.'

'I do. Tell me everything. I want to know.'

Miles hesitated before sitting down. Part of him regretted his confession. But a deeper part knew this was the moment he'd been waiting for. If he didn't confide in Isabel now, he never would, and he'd always regret it. So he told her about Francois Perigord's dirigible and Thomas Sheridan's box kite and a dozen other inventions, each of which got a little closer to the mystery of flight; and about the wayward genius of Tobias Smith and the mechanical efficiency of the English safety bicycle and the pelicans he'd watched riding the thermals as he wandered around the streets of Woolloomooloo. He was on his third whisky, and Isabel had poured herself another sherry and wanted to know where he stood on the woman question; and neither of them was listening to the other but both experienced a fuzzy pleasure in the other's company that her uncle couldn't fail to notice when he walked through the front door at ten minutes past eight, surprised that neither had taken the trouble to pick up the letter he'd left on the mantelpiece, which said that Isabel's grandmother was dying and she must come home at once.

The next morning, before breakfast, she was gone.

⤺

There was a page in Tobias Smith's notebook that Miles had never understood. It was a page about snakes. Now that Isabel was gone, Miles set about trying to unravel its meaning. The page was covered with muddled diagrams with arrows pointing in all directions and a text that wandered tortuously around the margins. Miles pored over it, transcribing and enlarging the diagrams while wrestling with Smith's chaotic handwriting. He was eager to see Isabel again, but at the same time he didn't want to see her with the mystery of the notebook only half solved.

The worst of winter was already over. The days were getting longer. One evening, while walking alone through the paddocks that lay behind the doctor's garden, Miles saw a carpet snake swim across a muddy dam. Watching from the bank, he noticed the pattern of ripples in the water caused by the undulations of its body. It was the same pattern he had been studying in Tobias Smith's notebook.

Smith had realised that the body of a swimming snake undulated sideways in order to propel the snake forwards. He made notes describing the same phenomenon in tadpoles and earthworms. Each displayed a characteristic side-to-side motion.

Eyeing the careless flap of a galah as it tumbled off a telegraph post, Smith had become convinced that the motion of the snake's body was a variation of the up-and-down motion of a bird's wing rotated by ninety degrees. From this he inferred that the most 'natural' form of aerial propulsion was not the wooden propeller advocated by European aviators, but some form of lateral reflex capable of mimicking these muscular contractions. A man-made flying machine, he concluded, would need to be powered by flappers.

It was only now, having seen the snake, that Miles understood what he meant. Reading the page again, he suddenly found that Smith's arcane diagrams made sense. One of them reminded him of the castanets that Mayfair had given him. He rummaged for them in the pockets of his coat. Now he knew what they were. There was a little toothed wheel at the back of each castanet that had often puzzled him, and a tiny hook. He had always thought of the wheel as frivolous, an ingenious adaptation that, when spun, caused the shells to rattle. He realised why the hook was there. Attached to a tightly wound rubber band, the whole apparatus would flutter. They were not castanets but flappers.

Miles walked to the window. Looking up at the bleached winter sky, he began to imagine a machine based on a series of box kites, powered by flappers hooked up to the chain wheel of an English safety bicycle.

The front door slammed. Galbraith always took some time wiping his shoes on the mat and putting on his claret-coloured leather slippers. Miles heard him wander down the hall to his study, then return a few minutes later. He called from the bottom of the stairs. 'A letter, young man,' he said.

Miles grabbed the notebook on his way down. The letter was from Isabel, a belated response to the two he'd written. 'Dearest Miles,' it said,

> I'm amazed that you have only written to me twice. I had expected to be written to weekly at least. I suppose I should be generous but I found your first letter rather obscure, and your second obscurer still. I hope my uncle is putting you to good use in the garden, and that your damage to the lawn is forgiven. My grandmother has risen from her death bed and vows to be with us for many years yet.
>
> Affectionately,
> Isabel

Miles read the letter several times while the doctor pottered back and forth in search of something he'd lost.

'No bad news, I hope,' he said.

Miles stuffed the letter in his trouser pocket. 'Isabel's grandmother is better.'

'That doesn't surprise me. She has, to my knowledge, been
on the verge of death at least twice in the past year. I suspect her
Maker beckons her only to lose His nerve at the prospect of her
coming. I'm not entirely sure that Isabel doesn't take after her in
some respects.'

Miles wrote back:

Dear Isabel,
I'll explain everything when I see you.

Yours,

M

It was the first week of August 1875. Miles's plaster was off;
the skin was pale and mottled like a trout. A slight lump indicated
where the break had been. With little to do in the garden, he went
to work on his box kites. On a low hill a mile from the doctor's
house, he proved that several kites joined together could fly as
one. By increasing the size of the biggest kite he was able to carry
heavier and heavier loads. One blustery morning he succeeded
in lifting a bag of oats weighing twenty pounds and keeping it
airborne for half an hour.

Sometimes the doctor came to watch, standing at a safe
distance with his hands buried deep in his pockets and a
quizzical look on his face. He liked to think of himself as
a modern man; he had a house full of gadgets intended to
make life easier or happier or less painful. One day, he imagined,
people would open their newspapers to find that a man
had learnt to fly. But it would not be in his lifetime and

the man would be humdrum and practical: an engineer or bicycle-maker. When he saw Tobias Smith's notebook it reminded him of the medieval mystics who sat in their cells conversing with the Holy Spirit. He tried to talk down Miles's expectations but succeeded only in making them bigger.

At the end of August Miles built his first man-lifter consisting of four kites strung together. In the paddock behind Macy's Hotel, watched by the doctor and a few bleary-eyed drinkers, he was hoisted twenty feet in the air and spent several minutes swinging in his harness before the wind dropped and he parachuted slowly to the ground. Exhilarated by his success, he decided to mount the two biggest kites on a timber frame. Among countless designs imagined by Smith, the shape Miles chose was a double crucifix, with a harness for himself beneath the larger kite. After failing several times to get the structure airborne, he cut away the vertical faces of both kites, creating two sets of parallel wings. He narrowly escaped serious injury when the glider took off unexpectedly, dragging him fifty yards before coming to rest in a wattle bush. On the second flight he held on, even attempting some basic manoeuvres in the few seconds he was airborne. The regulars at Macy's grew used to the sight of the young man floating between the eucalypts.

Another letter arrived from Sydney.

Dear Miles,
Visit me. I am bored.
Isabel

It took Miles a weekend to dismantle his kites. The doctor was sorry to see him go. They had grown fond of each other.

'You must have the bicycle,' he said.

Miles hesitated. Galbraith had already insisted on him taking ten pounds for his 'gardening'.

'Go on, my boy. Holsworthy did not make it with my anatomy in mind.'

They travelled together by coach to the railway station at Penrith with the bicycle rattling on the roof. It was a cold miserable morning. Their breath plumed the air as they shook hands on the platform. 'Give my love to Isabel,' said Galbraith.

As the train shuddered past the mansions overlooking the railway line, the homes of doctors and bankers and university men, Miles kept an eye out for the fig tree whose roots were slowly invading Isabel's living room. But there were scores of fig trees and dozens of mansions. To Miles McGinty, with his head in the clouds, one house looked just like another.

⌒

The poster was framed by two rusty drainpipes on a brick wall in Bathurst Street. Miles didn't notice it at first. He was watching the numbers above the shop doors. Galbraith had recommended an inexpensive boarding house run by Mrs Gursky, whose husband he had known on the goldfields.

As Miles hunted for the address, his gaze drifted to an umbrella shop whose side wall had been papered over with advertising posters. They merged into a formless smudge of black type on cheap paper. One, however, was darker than the rest, and it caught his eye. A pot-bellied silhouette was floating cross-legged three or four feet above the ground. Beneath the picture the wording said:

After his many Triumphs abroad,
MELCHIOR the ELECTRICIAN
Will Demonstrate his UNEARTHLY POWERS
at the Masonic Hall.
Doors Open at half past six.
Latecomers not Admitted.

Miles recognised the style at once. Wolunsky had substituted one of the magi for another. Balthasar the Levitator had been reincarnated.

Further up the hill was the place he'd been looking for: Mrs Gursky's Boarding House, for casual or long-term accommodation, rent payable in advance. He chose a sparsely furnished room at the back, paid ten shillings for a week's rent, parked his bicycle out the back and set off in search of Wolunsky.

The Masonic Hall was a squat brick building which gave the impression of having once aspired to grandeur before it was decided that the cost was too great. All that remained of its aspirations was a frieze above the entrance porch, which was now, like the rest of the building, covered with soot, pigeon droppings and other assorted deposits.

It was just after half past five. A noisy huddle of people stood at the side door, arguing over whether the man they had just seen was Melchior the Electrician or the caretaker. Miles stood close enough to listen, and to infer that the man they were talking about was either Wolunsky or someone pretending to be him.

He went round to the front door which was, to his surprise, open. An unwashed teacup and saucer on a table in the vestibule seemed to indicate that a doorkeeper had been on duty earlier in the day and was planning to return. But he was certainly not here now and Miles had no trouble finding his way past the main hall to a short corridor in which four doors faced each other in pairs. Two bore strange symbols, the third was a broom cupboard and the last had a ragged poster pinned to it. The smell of tobacco smoke crept under the gap. Miles put his ear to the door and heard a familiar wheezing sound. He knocked. There was a delay of several seconds before a voice called out, 'Enter.' Miles opened the door.

'So there you are, lad,' said Wolunsky. 'Been wondering when you'd turn up.'

At first Miles had difficulty recognising him. He was sitting in the middle of a worn, leather-covered horsehair sofa, smoking not his usual cheroot but a Havana cigar as big as a chair leg, the lightest puff of which spread a blanket of smoke thick enough to obscure not just Wolunsky himself but most of the wall behind.

'We got your letter,' he said. 'That is your mother got it and was kind enough to read it to me.'

Miles had expected there to be coolness between them. But Wolunsky was acting as though they'd parted on the best possible terms.

'Eliza'—Wolunsky stopped himself—'your mother and I were hoping you'd pay us a visit.' He stood up in a pair of tailored check trousers that, unlike any previous pair he had ever worn, fitted him to a tee. His shoes were patent leather; his shirt French linen. A gold chain hung from his waistcoat pocket. His hair had been cut, his yellow fingernails filed and even his eyebrows gave the impression of having been trimmed. A paunch pressed against the buttons of his waistcoat. His knuckles were still gnarled and swollen but there was a fat garnet ring on his little finger. Wolunsky had come into money, a great deal of it.

'A nice cut,' remarked Wolunsky, 'don't you agree?' He pointed at his trousers with the glowing end of his Havana. 'Jewish tailor in Chinatown. Odd combination, you'd have to say, but the fellow knows his business.'

Miles wondered if this was another of Wolunsky's illusions. But the gold was real enough; he could see the weight of the chain pulling on his pocket. 'You must be doing all right,' he said.

'All right is one word for it, lad. All right covers it handsomely.'

'Mother's well?' asked Miles.

'I think she'd admit to that. Yes, I think she probably would. No doubt about it, in fact.'

'Where is she?'

'Why, lad, where she's always been. That is she will be, when she gets here. A row or two from the back, just to keep an eye on things.' He took another grandiose puff on his cigar. 'A very dependable woman, your mother, as I'm sure you know.'

There was a lot that Miles had been itching to tell him: about the bicycle for a start. The old Wolunsky would have been keen to know all about it. His own art was so simple that it always amused him to hear about the props used by others. If there wasn't already a bicycling show somewhere in Australia, Miles was pretty sure there soon would be. But now he was embarrassed to mention it.

'Well,' said Wolunsky, 'aren't you going to ask how?'

'How what?'

'How the stocks of this modest enterprise have been transformed?'

A cloud of smoke concealed Wolunsky's retreat behind a Japanese screen. His act had become ornate since Miles had left. The cigar continued to burn by itself on a little round table in front of the sofa. Miles listened to the old wizard cursing behind the screen. He was having some trouble, whatever he was doing. 'Need any help?' he inquired mischievously.

Wolunsky didn't answer but emerged a moment later with a sinister-looking girdle around his middle and a large cushion stuffed down the back of his trousers. He waved the smoke away with his hands. 'The electro-magnetic corset,' he said. 'By God almighty, lad, you've never seen anything like it.'

That much was true. 'What is it?' Miles asked.

'What is it? I'll tell you what it is. It's the best tool a levitator ever got his dirty hands on, that's all. It's the alpha and the omega of levitation, the ant's pants is what it is. Just ask your mother. Had her eyes popping out of her head, it did.' He pulled the canvas straps tight, one around his waist and the other across his chest, securing them with sturdy brass buckles until he seemed ready to burst. 'If you wouldn't mind plugging me in, lad,' he said, handing Miles a pair of crocodile clips.

'To what?' asked Miles.

Wolunsky indicated a box on which he had previously been resting his feet. It was a grey metal thing about the size of a small suitcase. 'The dry cell,' he said.

Miles did as he was asked. Almost at once Wolunsky began to sway and shudder. He seemed to lose his balance but quickly regained it. Folding his arms across his chest, he shut his eyes and began to rise, just a few inches at first, then a couple of feet, his body as rigid as a stone buddha. The hard part was apparently over. He relaxed and scratched his nose.

'Well?' he said, winking his left eye. 'Can I take it you're impressed?'

Miles was astounded but wouldn't admit it. It certainly put

his bicycle in the shade, not to mention Sheridan's box kite. It made him wonder whether Wolunsky had been toying with him all those years. Miles was jealous. He reached down and unhitched one of the crocodile clips, bringing the levitator crashing to the floor.

'Very funny,' said Wolunsky, getting to his feet. He wasn't hurt. He had learnt that electricity was not to be trusted: hence the cushion.

'Are you going to tell me how it's done?' asked Miles.

'Do you *want* to know how it's done?' Wolunsky replied. 'I thought you'd put this hocus pocus behind you.'

Miles stared at him, as he remembered being stared at by Wolunsky that night on the stage of the Royal Victoria. 'I'm curious,' he said.

'Fair enough. The electricity in the coils energises the etheric matter that envelopes the body. Concentrate hard enough and the body rises of its own accord.'

'That's it? Put on the corset and fly?'

'In a nutshell,' said Wolunsky. 'Of course—'

'Why here?' asked Miles.

'Not big enough, you think? It suits me. Always preferred two small crowds to one big 'un. Though I must say, Eliza has a fancy we should be at the Theatre Royal.' He glanced at his watch. 'Is that the time, lad? I'll have to get a move on. Got to get the old make-up on.' He began unfastening his canvas straps.

Miles could hardly believe what he was hearing. 'Make-up?'

Wolunsky wriggled about like a snake shucking off its skin. 'Your mother's idea,' he said. 'Thought it would add a bit of mystery.'

'And the name?' asked Miles.

'The Electrician? Hers. Good, isn't it? Came up with it on our honeymoon.' He bit his lip as the corset clattered around his feet. Miles's mouth fell open.

Wolunsky picked up the stub of his cigar and puffed on it shyly. 'We got married, lad.'

Eliza was exactly where Wolunsky said she'd be, a row or two from the back, a couple of seats in, close enough to the aisle to help out if she was needed. 'Miles!' she cried. 'How…never mind, never mind, come here.' She stood up and threw her arms around his neck. 'You've seen…' She could see he had. 'Did he…I told him not to…Oh, Miles.' People were shuffling crab-like to their seats. 'You'll stay, won't you?'

'I wouldn't miss it,' said Miles.

'You're not cross?'

'That you're married? No.' He felt self-conscious and sat down. 'Would it matter if I was?'

Eliza was fiddling with the pleats of her peacock-blue dress. 'Not really, dear. We can't undo it now, can we? Anyway, Zbigniew's made an honest woman of me.' She lowered her voice, though not by much. 'About time, I suppose.'

Miles had intended to tell her about Isabel but the news seemed banal. He found it hard to imagine Wolunsky as his stepfather.

'How long have you been here?' asked Eliza. In the half-light his face reminded her so much of his father that she had to look away. 'Miles, darling, if only you'd written.'

'I did write.'

'Once. I don't call that writing. Where are you staying? Not the Orient?'

'Bathurst Street. Gursky's.'

'You can't. You must stay with us. Please, Miles. You're not married, are you? Don't tell me you're married.'

'I'm not married.'

She stood up suddenly. 'Oh God, Miles, let's leave. He can do without me for an evening. We can't talk here.'

'But the demonstration—'

She bent down to speak in his ear. This time it was just between them. 'It's the same old stuff,' she whispered, 'only grander.'

They didn't go to any of the expensive restaurants where Eliza and Wolunsky were now honoured guests; not even to the Orient Hotel, where they could have eaten for nothing and where Eliza would certainly have been petitioned for a short recital; but to one of the tap rooms on Kent Street where they attracted no more notice than the drunks steaming beside the fire. And while Wolunsky floated in his electro-magnetic corset, Miles told his mother as much as he wanted her to know.

'Is she clever, Miles?'

'Who?'

'Your friend Isabel. She sounds clever.'

'I suppose you'd call her that.'

'But rather...unconventional.'

'Probably.'

'She's not a vegetarian, is she?'

'What?'

'It was in the newspaper. They live on nothing but potatoes.'

Miles buttoned up his beaver coat. 'I must go, Mother.'

'You'll stay this time, won't you?' There was something almost desperate in her voice. 'Poor Mr Wolunsky was quite despondent after you left.'

'He seems to have got over it.'

'He has a good heart, Miles,' she said. 'I really consider myself quite fortunate.'

'Don't worry,' said Miles. 'I'm not going anywhere.'

~

The size of the Dowling mansion took him by surprise. It was much bigger than Isabel had led him to believe. Its red-brick walls and turreted roof suggested a raffish welcome. Miles rode from Bathurst Street on his bicycle. The crunch of its rubber tyres on the gravel path drew Isabel running to the sitting-room window.

'Miles,' she called out, 'is that you?'

'Were you expecting someone else?' he asked. He noticed an elderly servant staring at him from an upstairs window.

Isabel was unusually sheepish. She had let slip a careless remark about Miles and the awkward look on her mother's face had told her not to mention him again. She wanted to hug Miles at the door, then thought better of it. Shaking his hand seemed ridiculous, so she shouted up to Matilda that she was going for a walk. Matilda called back but the door was already shut.

'Your handwriting's terrible,' she said. 'I could hardly read your letters.'

They were still standing on the porch. 'I'm not much of a writer,' replied Miles. 'Are we going somewhere?'

Isabel began walking down the path towards the road.

'Shall I leave this?' asked Miles.

'No. Bring it. It's all downhill.'

'And uphill on the way back?'

'I suppose so.' They walked for a while in silence with Miles wheeling the bicycle between them. 'Of course,' she said, 'we could always ride it.' She eyed the double-sprung saddle. 'You could sit on that bit and I could sit on…this bit. Or the other way round.'

'I don't like our chances,' said Miles.

You might be surprised,' she replied.

Miles held the bicycle for her to get on. 'You told me it was downhill all the way.'

'Did I?'

Isabel was indignant to find she couldn't turn the pedals. 'Go on then,' she said. 'You do it.'

Miles climbed into the saddle. Isabel perched on the crossbar. Miles reached around her to the handlebars and began to pedal. He noticed that the freckles on her nose had faded. Her hair smelt different.

'Am I heavy?' she asked.

'Light as a feather,' he lied.

Smoke poured from the chimneys of the prussic acid factory at Iron Cove. The tide was out. The mud bristled with mangrove roots. Miles propped the bicycle against a tree and they wandered along the foreshore.

'I needn't ask if you missed me,' said Isabel.

'I was coming back anyway,' replied Miles.

'That's a lie,' she laughed. 'You came to see me.'

A pelican was squatting on a sandbar, its head submerged in its wing feathers.

'You don't talk much, do you?' said Isabel.

Miles didn't answer. He was thinking.

'I talk all the time,' she went on. 'I can't help it. Do you mind?'

'Why should I?'

'I got it from my mother. It's the only thing I inherited from her. Papa's as closed as an oyster.' She glanced at Miles. 'You're thinking. I can tell. Any moment you're going to say something.'

Miles said nothing. They walked on. 'Hurry up, Miles,' she said at last. 'The anticipation is killing me.'

'There was a newspaper man,' said Miles.

Isabel hung back.

'Lived in Chicago,' Miles went on, 'near the meatworks. He spent his days reporting the comings and goings of ships on Lake Michigan. But all his life he dreamed of flying.'

Isabel followed a few paces behind. If there was to be a story, she wanted her share of it. 'His name,' she said, 'was Joseph Bridges.'

'He lived by himself,' said Miles.

'No,' she corrected him. 'He had a wife called Maria.'

Miles glared at her over his shoulder. He was not going to let himself be pushed out of his own story. 'He'd survived polio as a boy. It had left him with one leg shorter than the other.'

Isabel was prepared to compromise. 'Maria died suddenly,' she said. 'Joseph woke up one morning and found her perfectly still beside him. The doctors said it was a brain haemorrhage. It had probably been coming for years. Maria was lucky to have survived so long. She didn't suffer. But Joseph did. He was angry with her for leaving him.'

Miles stood and waited for her to catch up. 'Why?' he demanded.

'Joseph was terrified of the sea,' said Isabel. It wasn't her intention to wrest the tale from him, only to let him know she was there. She'd always been an active listener, interrupting her father's bedtime stories.

'Don't be stupid,' snapped Miles. 'He spent his life on the docks.'

'He was terrified of the sea,' insisted Isabel. 'He watched the ships sailing away to Rio de Janeiro and Hamburg and London and longed to visit those places but he knew he'd die without seeing them. Maria understood his fear and used to read aloud books by great travellers so he could imagine the places he would never see. And though he blamed his wife for leaving him, the truth was he was angry with himself.'

Miles was beginning to lose the thread. 'Bridges,' he said crossly, 'watched the seagulls wheeling over the big schooners and imagined being one of them, looking out across the great lakes at the islands and continents that lay over the horizon.

'One night,' he continued, 'a fire broke out in one of the bond stores. The warehouse was full of property that had been left behind or confiscated over the years. The morning after the fire Bridges noticed an old French velocipede standing among the ashes. Nobody arrived to claim it, and a few days later he decided to take it home.'

Miles expected Isabel to be mystified. But she'd won forty pounds on a velocipede and wasn't going to let this one beat her. 'The machine had buckled in the heat,' she said.

'But the moving parts,' countered Miles, 'were miraculously

intact and Joseph soon discovered how it worked. The rider's feet rested on swinging cranks which moved a pair of iron rods linked to levers mounted on either side of the rear wheel. When the rider pumped his legs, the cranks pulled the levers and the wheel turned. Bridges discovered that its creator, a man named Martineau, had invented the velocipede only after his wife stopped his experiments with flying machines. He wondered whether the wheels were just a disguise, and paid a local shipbuilder to make him a tin propeller. Then he built a pair of wings.'

'You've left out the sisters,' said Isabel.

'He didn't have any.'

'But she did.'

Miles looked at her doubtfully. At last he said, 'Maria had two sisters.'

'Five,' said Isabel, 'and they all loved their brother-in-law. They couldn't bear to see him living alone and quarrelled over which of them should marry him. They didn't know anything about his plans to build a flying machine.'

'If they had,' said Miles, 'they'd have had nothing to do with him.'

'Who knows?' Isabel retorted. 'They might have loved him even more.'

'It was Rachel, the youngest, who married him.'

'No,' said Isabel. 'It was Lydia, the eldest.'

The pelican looked up as they passed. It seemed to contemplate flying off before paddling to the edge of the sandbar and dipping its huge beak in the water.

'Bridges,' he continued, 'had always kept a diary alongside his professional notebooks. But after Maria's death the two became confused and some entries found their way into the wrong book. Amid the columns of shipping details, his notebook for 1870 contained several pages of erotic verse about Maria.'

Isabel took over. 'One day he made the mistake of leaving it open for Lydia to read. She was a jealous woman. Rather than destroy one notebook, Lydia incinerated them all.'

'The loss of his poems,' said Miles, 'was bad enough, but forty years of his life was recorded in those shipping details. With Maria gone and his notebooks burnt, Bridges felt he'd been robbed of everything. He shut himself away with his flying machine—'

'But he couldn't build it on his own,' said Isabel. 'Day after day, Lydia stood at the window watching him. She was ashamed of what she'd done. Sometimes, late at night, she crept into his shed and, gently rocking the cranks, felt the propeller spin. As she was by far the stronger of the two, it must have seemed obvious, even to Joseph, that she should be the one to fly it.'

'But she was pregnant,' interrupted Miles.

'Though early in her term,' said Isabel, 'and bursting with vigour.'

'One morning,' he said, 'they dragged the velocipede plane to where the banks of the lake were steep. As the wind picked up, the wings began to tear at their moorings. There was only one harness and neither would give it up—'

'Both,' said Isabel, 'fearing the loss of the other.'

'As they quarrelled,' said Miles, 'over who should be the one to fly, the machine began to roll down the slope, accelerating as it approached the bank. The momentum caused the cranks to rise and fall by themselves. The propeller started spinning...'

'And the velocipede,' said Isabel, 'took off without them.'

'Do you always insist on having the last word?' asked Miles.
'Always,' said Isabel.

Miles bought a pair of brand-new boots and presented himself
at the door of the Royal Victoria Theatre, where Briggs hired him
on the spot in his former role of flyman, scene-painter, set-shifter
and odd-job man. He now had his workshop back. With twenty-
five shillings in his pocket every week, Miles moved to a larger
room and put himself down for Mrs Gursky's hot breakfast of
porridge, fried kidneys and toast, delivered on a tray at half past
six every morning.

He had already begun experimenting with flappers powered
by stretched rubber bands. His flapper-driven biplane #1, fitted
with eight rubber bands, was three and a half feet long and made
of timber rods and stretched linen. It was too flimsy to fly but
formed the basis of flapper-driven biplane #2, which used sixteen
rubber bands connected via ivory pulleys and brass toggles to a
pair of linen flappers. This model took two months to build. It
flew a hundred and sixty feet along the beach at Maroubra before
veering out to sea and being smashed to pieces in the surf.

The first weeks of summer were taken up with the construc-
tion of flapper-driven biplane #3, powered by twenty-four rubber
bands. The flappers were moved by steel cranks and the wings,
for the first time, were curved, which dramatically improved the
lift. Biplane #3 flew two hundred and sixteen feet and landed
safely on a pair of skids.

As the new year approached, Miles started work on biplane
#4. In a huge storeroom beneath the stage of the Royal Victoria

Theatre he cleared space for a full-sized machine that canni-
balised Holsworthy's pedal-and-chain assembly to work four
canvas flappers. Miles would lie on his front, pedalling by hand
and operating a wooden rudder with his feet.

Three times a week Isabel left the house in Stanmore with a
leather satchel containing her palette and sketchbook, supposedly
bound for the Lebovic art school in King Street, only to get off
the omnibus three stops early and head instead for the Royal
Victoria Theatre.

There was no shortage of canvas for the wings. Briggs was
fastidious about his backdrops, insisting on a new sky for every
show. The canvas could be painted over several times before it
became too difficult to work on. Rolls and rolls of discarded
material lay under the stage, trembling skyscapes into which Miles
had poured all he knew about clouds and winds and storms.
Miles and Isabel used white chalk to mark up the yards of canvas
they needed to wrap the wings and tailplane. He cut and she
stitched.

It took them all summer. By March the machine was
finished. With Miles pedalling as hard as he could, the flappers
sounded like the thrashing wings of a caged bird. They kicked up
clouds of chalk. When the dust settled Miles looked as though
he'd been rolled in flour.

'You're as white as a ghost,' laughed Isabel.

At the western corner of Circular Quay stood the Belmore Hotel,
a tin-roofed building whose washing, strung on two lines over a
tiny cobbled courtyard, was clearly visible from the street. Further

up the hill an enormous painted sign, streaked with grime, marked the site of the Hotel Metropole, where a decent pot of tea and muffins could be had for two and sixpence, accompanied by the strains of a Russian violinist.

Miles and Isabel went there from time to time, when it rained and they got tired of being splashed by omnibuses, or when Isabel was in a mood to listen to the sad Russian fiddler, or when they were out of sorts and could stare at each other sullenly over the decrepit crockery.

They were having tea one Saturday afternoon at a corner table near the window. Isabel was fingering an English cigarette. The tables were so small their knees touched. Isabel disliked the taste of the cigarette but she'd made such a fuss of lighting it that some of the waiters were now watching her and she felt obliged to smoke it to the end. Miles's hands, she noticed, were blistered from the hours he'd spent practising in his harness. The wings were finished. Miles had built a simple tricycle undercarriage. All that had to be done was for the pieces to be assembled. But something was holding him back.

Most of Isabel's attention was on the cigarette. She sipped at her tea. They'd run out of things to say. Then a man's voice addressed her: 'Isabel.'

She dropped her cigarette. It was Windsor.

'What a pleasant—' The schoolmaster stopped in mid-sentence as he grasped the situation that chance had thrown his way. Here, in the company of a young man to whom she was obviously not married, was the daughter of his sister's husband's cousin, a girl who'd done her best to slight him while they resided under the same roof; who'd paid scant attention to his lectures, flouted his advice, mocked his principles and finally contrived a humiliating scene that made it impossible for him to stay. It took him longer to remember the face of the person she was with, but slowly it dawned on him that this was the insolent youth—the would-be aeronaut—with whom he'd argued on the coach from Katoomba. He had perhaps even disparaged the boy over dinner. Here, then, was an irony to savour. The two were undoubtedly lovers meeting in secret. Windsor moistened his lips in anticipation.

The fact of having come upon them together was so fortuitous that he was tempted to believe it was divinely inspired. It quite blinded him to the potential embarrassment of being found there himself, preparing to strike a bargain with one of the tarts who conducted business from the lounge of the Metropole.

'You are well, I see,' said Windsor, determined to prolong his enjoyment.

Isabel didn't answer. She had done nothing wrong but the sight of him was so odious that she felt somehow soiled.

'And you, young man, have we not had the pleasure of meeting?'

Miles remembered the face but couldn't place it.

'Windsor,' said the pedagogue, extending his sallow hand. 'And you are?'

'Miles McGinty.'

The word 'McGinty' meant nothing to Windsor personally. He did not go to the theatre; he considered it immoral. But he had read the name often enough in the newspapers and knew the old gossip about Eliza and her lovers. He had heard that her boy was a bastard.

'McGinty?' he said. 'Would you by any chance be related to the actress of that name?'

'She's my mother,' he answered.

The pedagogue seemed to shiver at this renewed proof of God's favour. Returning to Isabel, he said, 'I trust your parents are in good health?'

'Yes.'

'And your dear sisters?'

This time Isabel didn't reply. She noticed again the translucency of his skin, the way his veins pulsed on the backs of his hands. 'What do you want?' she demanded.

'Me, my dear? Nothing. Nothing at all.'

'Perhaps he wants a muffin,' said Miles.

Windsor smiled thinly.

'Then leave us alone,' said Isabel.

He stood warming himself, like a lizard, in front of the window, then turned and departed without another word.

Miles and Isabel sat for a long time staring across the table. Their tea was cold. They had looked at each other so often yet they saw something now that neither had seen before, or that both had seen and neither had expressed. 'He thinks we're lovers,' said Isabel. 'He's going to tell my parents.'

'You can deny it,' Miles said.

'But perhaps we are,' Isabel said, reaching for his hand.

Neither of them spoke. A ribbon of smoke unwound from Isabel's neglected cigarette. Miles was smiling as he put five shillings on the table. Not long after, they tiptoed up the iron staircase to Miles's narrow room on the first floor of Mrs Gursky's boarding house. He undid the top two buttons of Isabel's dress and felt suddenly shy.

'Don't stop,' she whispered.

'Mr Windsor,' said Mrs Dowling.

The pedagogue's normally waxy complexion was flushed from the summer heat. His Melton overcoat was still buttoned to the throat. He had come by hansom cab and almost capered up the gravel path to the house.

'May I come in?' he asked.

'My husband is not at home,' she said, declining his proffered hand.

'I have some intelligence, madam, that it would be to your advantage to hear.'

'Intelligence?'

'It concerns your daughter Isabel.'

'She's not hurt, is she?'

Windsor unfastened the top button of his overcoat. 'That will be for you to judge. If you would like my opinion—'

But Mrs Dowling did not want his opinion, only his news, and for that she was obliged to let him through the door.

'Eliza McGinty?' said Dowling, scratching his ear. 'Did we not see her Hamlet?'

'For heaven's sake, Ernest. The boy with whom Isabel has been corresponding—'

'His name is Miles, if I'm not mistaken.'

'I don't care what his name is. He's her illegitimate child. And he's seducing our daughter.'

'Isabel is not fifteen, my dear. I dare say the young man does not make an exhibition of his parentage. She survived without us once. Shouldn't we now allow her to choose her own company?'

'It is not hers to choose. This liaison will disgrace us all. We have six daughters, in case you'd forgotten.'

'The fellow is not seducing all of them.' He paused. 'Is he?'

'Don't be an idiot, Ernest. One is bad enough.'

Dowling remained sceptical. 'Windsor reported this?'

'Yes.'

'And what do you imagine he was doing in the Hotel Metropole?'

'I didn't ask him.'

Dowling recalled hearing from a colleague some allusion to prostitutes in the Metropole but this was not something he could repeat to his wife. 'Having tea?' he said.

'I beg your pardon?'

'Windsor says he saw Isabel and the young man having tea?'

'I told you he did.'

'And you take this as evidence of seduction?'

'Isabel has been carrying on a liaison behind our backs. The boy's mother is an actress. He is illegitimate. Must I spell it out?'

'I understood, my dear, that she was quite fond of him.' Dowling paused to consider the wisdom of what he was about to say. 'Are you sure we are justified in holding the boy's birth against him? I'm sure Isabel…' He saw how the sentence was going to be received and left it unfinished. 'Is she upstairs?' he asked. 'I will speak to her.'

'I've already spoken to her,' said Louisa. 'There is no necessity for you to repeat it.'

'Repeat what exactly?'

'That she will not see him again.'

'Of course. And did she agree?'

'No. But she will.'

Her husband scratched his ear again. 'I don't see how we can enforce that, Louisa.'

The use of her first name in conversation was so rare that Mrs Dowling's eyes opened wide. 'I have explained to her,' she said, 'that she will be cut off without a penny. That will bring her to her senses.'

Dowling had learnt not to challenge his wife on the matter of his daughters' upbringing. It was understood between them that his own contribution dwindled inexorably after the girls reached the age of five. Once they were fifteen it was judged to be irrelevant. He accepted this, but at the same time he felt he owed it to his youngest daughter to speak. He knew that Isabel was not like her sisters. 'I rather doubt,' he said, 'that we can buy her obedience.'

'Just watch,' said Mrs Dowling.

Dowling had a firm but unspoken faith in his youngest daughter's morals, but it was not the sort that could be set against his wife's panic at the collapse of her plans for Isabel's marriage. A stronger willed man might have given in less easily or not at all. Dowling, however, had reached an age where peace served a deeper need in him than principle. He had seen his wife's temper and did not want to see it again. He was prepared to sacrifice Miles to avoid it. And so, despite his qualms, he did.

'You will back me up, Ernest,' she said. It did not sound like a question.

'You said he was dead.'

It was half past four in the morning. Isabel had slipped out of the house for the first time in a week and walked the three miles to Mrs Gursky's boarding house.

Miles knew at once who she was talking about. 'He's dead to us,' he said.

'It was a lie, Miles.'

Barefoot and half-asleep, Miles said nothing. The sky was just beginning to lighten. He stood aside to let her in but Isabel didn't move. 'Why didn't you tell me?' she asked.

'Why do you think?'

'Probably, Miles, because you were stupid enough to think that I'd want nothing to do with you if I knew.'

'I don't imagine there are many bastards at your mother's Sunday lunches.'

'None, I should think. They might be livelier if there were.'

'Windsor told them?'

'Of course Windsor told them. And they told me.'

Miles wanted to ask Isabel to forgive him, only the betrayal was not his but his father's. He couldn't meet her gaze. 'What now, then?' he asked.

'Are you going to let me in,' she said, 'or are you going to make love to me on the landing?'

∼

A passenger ship, the *Aurora*, was sitting at Circular Quay. She had come all the way from London with a cargo of felt hats, candles and carpets and was returning via the Americas. She wasn't large and she wasn't comfortable but there were cabins available and the captain, a genial old Swede, was happy enough to take them, and even to marry them. Isabel still had the forty pounds she'd won. She would have eloped with nothing but Miles hesitated.

A fortnight went by. Now that she was forbidden, Isabel saw more of Miles than ever. Her mother was a stern but not an effective gaoler. Isabel was too resourceful to be kept at home. The *Aurora* sailed without them but there were plenty of other ships. There were trains. There were coaches. There were steamers dawdling daily down the Parramatta River. Miles kept making excuses. They had a hundred opportunities to make their escape.

Isabel grew anxious. 'Is it me?' she asked.

'Is what you?'

They were sitting under a cypress tree in the botanic gardens. The morning sun was sparkling on the harbour. 'We can't sneak around for ever,' she said.

Miles squeezed her hand. 'I can't go.'

She couldn't hide her impatience. She knew what was coming.

'I've got to know if it flies,' said Miles.

'Come on then,' she said. 'What are we waiting for?'

She made it sound as ordinary as riding a tram. Miles thought for a moment she was making fun of him. It was true she had hoped to avoid this scene, to delay it, perhaps indefinitely. But she saw now that it was inevitable. They would be incomplete without it.

'It's Sunday. The theatre's locked,' said Miles.

'Then we'll unlock it.'

Finding a cart for hire on the Sabbath was not easy, but a five-pound note solved the problem. By midday Miles had the pieces of his biplane #4 loaded onto a dray, and by twenty past he and Isabel and a driver in a leather waistcoat were trundling up Oxford Street. An hour later they came over the brow of the hill that ran down to Clovelly.

Behind the cliffs a small paddock sloped towards the sea. Miles was banking on this to provide the momentum for his flying machine to become airborne. On the far side of a two-rail fence, a wattle wound filigree shadows over the cracked brown soil. A few cattle lay on the grass, slapping blowflies with their tails. The sea was blue and sluggish.

For another five pounds the carter was happy to help them unload. He didn't ask what the stuff was for. Over the years he'd carried everything from pianos to corpses; he'd learnt not to be curious. He stuffed the money in his leather waistcoat and didn't look back.

Isabel couldn't help laughing at his eagerness to be gone. Miles wondered what was so funny. She had awaited her opportunity and now it was here she was almost frightened to take it. Had she left it too late? What if Miles wouldn't listen? 'In a town on the edge of the desert,' she began, 'there lived two lovers.'

Miles was bolting the canvas wings to the fuselage. He wasn't in the mood to hear a story. 'Hold this,' he said, putting a wrench in her hand.

'The town was in Arabia. His name was Murzuk and he was a slave; hers was Jeshri and she was the only daughter of Shakhbut the sultan. They lived in a stone castle built on an escarpment. Beneath them salt flats ran out to the sea, but the haze was so thick no-one could tell where the salt flats ended and the sea began.'

Miles pretended not to be listening. One of the flappers had been knocked crooked and needed straightening.

'Shakhbut the sultan was a great collector of birds. Each year he sent Murzuk to capture the falcons that flew along the coast at the beginning of winter. He was fonder of them than he was of his daughter. When they were sick he had Murzuk give them purges of sugar and egg yolks mixed with milk. Sometimes Jeshri was allowed to watch. She saw how gently Murzuk nursed the birds, how cleverly he mended their broken feathers with slivers of gazelle horn. If no-one was listening she spoke to him and he spoke quietly back. In time they fell in love. But while they remained in her father's castle they could never be alone.'

'So they escaped,' said Miles. He saw the story becoming weighed down with detail. He wanted to hurry her along.

'Of course they escaped,' she said.

'How?' A faint smile reassured her.

'A party of Arabs had arrived in town with twenty falcons trained for the lure. Besides the falcons they brought a hundred kites and eagles, all ringed and hooded. The hawking season was about to begin so Murzuk was sent by his master to discover whether the birds were for sale. One of the Arabs was a silver-haired old man called Zayid who had been a slaver in his youth. He remembered the day when he had sold a dozen boys to Shakhbut's father. The memory of it now made him ashamed. He agreed to sell his birds cheaply but only on condition that Murzuk be given to him for a month to be taught the secrets of handling them.'

Miles had succeeded in loosening the flapper and was now attempting to thread the chain over the chain wheel. He was still listening.

'At once,' said Isabel, 'Jeshri saw their chance to escape

together. But Murzuk hesitated. He was afraid of being betrayed and recaptured, since Shakhbut would undoubtedly have him tortured to death. Speaking to the old man, and seeing the hooded birds, had reminded him of a tale in which a camel was carried off by a thousand kites to punish its adulterous owner. The castle was surrounded by wells and grazing land that drew kites from the neighbouring desert. Murzuk soon had a hundred birds of his own, each of which he tethered with a woven cord thread. "The birds," he told Jeshri, "will carry us to freedom."'

'She didn't trust him,' said Miles. Looking up, he thought Isabel had never looked lovelier. Her cheeks were flushed. Her hair flew like sand blowing off a dune.

'How could she?' Isabel replied. 'She reminded him it was a fable; no-one had ever witnessed a camel taken by kites. But Murzuk was consumed by the idea. He dreamt of nothing else. He was passionate and pig-headed and couldn't conceive he might be wrong. And Jeshri loved him. She had never loved anyone else. Sometimes she almost believed his plan would work.

'One morning just before dawn they climbed together to the highest tower of the sultan's castle. It was winter and bitterly cold. In the courtyard below, they heard fires crackling and saw slaves carrying cauldrons of rice and bowls of milk from the goat shed. Murzuk had made them each a leather girdle in which the kites would carry them out over the salt flats and across the straits to Persia. He was in high spirits and if Jeshri was frightened, she didn't show it.'

Miles had his back to her. She couldn't see his face. Her fingers brushed his neck.

'Murzuk,' she said, 'tied a sheepskin of water around his waist. One by one he slipped the hoods from the kites. As the sun rose, they held each other and stepped off the tower. The tethered kites climbed with a soft thrashing sound and for a moment the lovers dissolved in the mist between the salt flats and the sea.'

The machine perched on three wheels, nose up, a baggy-throated vulture surveying the ocean. The afternoon was a scorcher, a hundred and ten and not a scrap of shade. A hot wind ruffled the wings. The painted clouds trembled in the haze.

The little beach was deserted. The rotting carcass of a shark had been carried over the rocks at the mouth of the bay and washed up on the sand.

'Wait,' cried Isabel.

A travelling photographer was wheeling his portable darkroom down the hill. He noticed the shark lying on the beach, walked over to it, then turned around and started trudging back towards the cemetery at Waverley. Sunday was always good for mourners.

'We must have a picture,' she said.

The photographer was persuaded to set up his tripod in the corner of the paddock. He was a portrait man and had never had much luck with landscapes.

'We're not after the scenery,' said Isabel.

'The sun's too bloody bright,' the photographer complained. 'The wind's too bloody dry. I'll never get me emulsions down in this bloody heat.' He stared suspiciously at the aeroplane. 'What's it for?' he asked.

'Watch,' said Isabel.

Isabel had given him precise instructions: where to point the camera, when to take the picture, where to deliver it. He printed the names in his book: Mr and Mrs E. Dowling of 9 Railway Avenue, Stanmore; Melchior and Mrs McGinty, The Orient Hotel, Sydney; and Dr Galbraith of Emu Plains. 'That's six quid,' he said hopefully. She gave him ten. A crooked smile settled on his lips.

'The lovers...' said Miles. 'Did they reach Persia?'

'I don't know,' she answered.

Isabel squinted at the sky. There wasn't a cloud in sight.

'Where are you going to land?' she asked.

Miles pointed down the scalloped coastline. The beach at Coogee was wide enough though he didn't fancy the rocks. Perhaps the sand was softer at Maroubra. He was hoping to put the aeroplane down undamaged.

He looked so pale and gangly in a crumpled shirt and moleskin trousers tied like a sack around his thin waist. Fear and excitement had drained the colour from his face.

That was when Isabel decided. 'Kiss me, Miles,' she said. She gripped him tight. She could feel his heart racing.

'Get a move on,' shouted the photographer. 'I've got a bloody plate going off here.'

As Miles wriggled into his harness, Isabel calmly pulled the blocks from the wheels. The machine began to roll downhill. Miles looked over his shoulder. 'What are you doing?'

She lay down beside him. 'I'm coming too.' There was only one harness and Miles was wearing it. The aeroplane was gathering speed. Isabel wound a leather strap around her right wrist; her left hand gripped one of the wooden spars. Miles was pedalling as hard as he could. The four canvas flappers beat the air behind him. The hot wind seared his face. Isabel felt the vibrations of the wheels as they bumped along the ground. She held her breath as the wheels went over the edge and the curved wings bowed and filled with air.

For a few moments the machine seemed to hang motionless. Their stomachs heaved as a great gust of wind took them. The canvas flapped around their ears. Isabel looked back at the little photographer hunched under his black cloth. The coastline unfurled beneath them. Miles felt an enormous relief. Isabel held on for her life. 'Don't stop,' she whispered.

Far below, the photographer thought he heard laughter.

The old century limped to an end. Crowds still gathered to see Wolunsky; not at the Royal Victoria Theatre or even the Masonic Hall, but on warm afternoons in a quiet corner of the Domain. He was eighty-five, but his tales were as haunting as ever and his cockiness not altogether gone.

The years had made him feeble. Some days his hips seized up and he couldn't get out of bed. Other mornings it took him a quarter of an hour just to put on his socks. Without Eliza to look after him—and she was nearly eighty herself—Wolunsky would have felt there was little to live for.

Most afternoons found him nursing a fat cigar on the verandah of the Orient Hotel, reminiscing over the days when he'd squatted on rickety stools in Bible-bashers' tents and sawdust pubs while a scrawny child floated in the glare of a gas lamp. Eliza sat beside him letting her tea turn cold as she squinted at the newspaper. She searched for familiar names among the obituaries or simply let her thoughts wander over the stages, big and small, where she'd declaimed the speeches of Hamlet and Mother Goose. From time to time she'd stare at the sky, hoping to catch a glimpse of something, a speck or blur that hadn't been there before.

They comforted each other in their way.

'Over here, ladies. Plenty of room in the shade.' Wolunsky's voice was thin and weary but he still had a touch of the showman. His eyes hadn't lost their sparkle. He was standing in a corner of the Domain under the wrinkled elbow of a Moreton Bay fig. Its roots hung over him like the tassles of a curtain. A small crowd was watching, ten or a dozen souls drawn by the sight of a wizened old man in a cape. Eliza was sitting a little way off, her face almost hidden beneath a wide-brimmed hat. Between them stood a small table covered by a tatty velvet cloth. There was something under it, a box or frame of some sort. A sharp corner poked through a tear in the cloth. It was the last week of December 1903.

Wolunsky began, as ever, circumspectly. Old age had made his stories leaner, more elliptical. He no longer had the breath to spare on unnecessary patter. 'There was a young bloke,' he said, 'willowy, restless, an only son. He dreamt all his life of flying. Talked of nothing else. Read everything there was to read on the subject. Handy with a hammer and saw. Wasn't afraid of a few bruises. The boy decided to build a flying machine.'

'Where?' asked a man in a cinnamon coat.

'Here,' Wolunsky answered.

'Was he a mate of yours?'

'Does it make any difference?'

The man shook his head. 'Just curious.'

Wolunsky struck a match and set fire to the Havana he'd been rolling between his knobbly fingers. These days it was as much as he could do to draw the smoke out of it; it no longer went down into his lungs but sat in his mouth, weaving through the gaps in his teeth. He glanced over his shoulder at Eliza, as if waiting to be prompted. The story belonged to both of them now. It kept them alive.

He went on, 'He'd read about the French and their propellers and decided they'd got it arse about. Watched the birds and reckoned an aeroplane would need flappers to fly. Common enough mistake. He wasn't the first.'

'Was he married?' asked a woman in a black crepe dress.

There was a time when Wolunsky hated being interrupted. It distracted him, made him forget what was coming next. These days he depended on it. 'There was a girl,' he answered. 'She had white skin, green eyes, freckles on her nose, a figure to make you weep.'

'And they were in love?'

'Head over heels,' said Wolunsky.

The woman smiled. She'd been young once. She hadn't forgotten.

'The flying machine,' he went on, 'was as good as built. She helped him finish it. He reckoned a half decent breeze could carry them all the way to New Zealand.'

'Why New Zealand?' the man in the cinnamon coat wanted to know.

Wolunsky shrugged. It could have been anywhere. He was nearing the end. 'The girl wasn't keen,' he said, 'but she could see his heart was set on it.'

'She refused to be left behind,' the woman suggested.

Wolunsky removed the cigar from his mouth and flicked a cone of ash from the tip. 'She thought they'd be lucky to get off the ground at all. They hauled the machine to a paddock at the top of a cliff.'

Eliza gazed at him from under her floppy hat. She had lost a lover and after that a son, both vanished into thin air. Now there was just Wolunsky. He looked tired. He'd been standing too long. She gestured to him to sit down. There was no hurry. The story wasn't going anywhere.

A bespectacled man asked if there was some sort of proof.

Resting his cigar on the corner of the table, Wolunsky gently removed the cloth from a faded picture in a black frame. 'A travelling photographer happened to be passing. He'd seen the machine from a distance and thought it might be worth a picture. Perhaps he could sell it to the newspapers. He arrived in the nick of time.' The crowd moved closer.

'I can't see anything,' said the bespectacled man.

Wolunsky pointed with a shaky finger to a mass of cloud at the edge of the picture. There were two dark smudges. It wasn't much to remember them by.

'There's nothing there,' said the man in the coat.

'I see a blur,' said the short-sighted one. 'It could be something.'

The woman in crepe glanced at Eliza. 'Such strange clouds,' she said. 'You'd think they were painted.'

Wolunsky picked up his cigar and let the smoke dissolve among the branches.